SEEKER'S REVOLUTION

Book Three of the Seeker's Trilogy

CASSANDRA BOYSON

DEDICATED TO

God, the love of my life

CONTENTS

PREFACE

"THE TIME DRAWS NEAR," said a large winged creature with five piercing eyes.

"When it will be determined whether for the next thousand years the Greater Archipelagos will be cursed or favored," said another creature of the assembled group who always finished the winged creature's sentences.

"Yes, I have seen," said one with a long, brilliant green beard and glistening bronze skin. He knelt over a time-line on the floor of the Great One's throne room. "Something must be done."

"Someone must be sent, of course, and soon," said another matter-of-factly. This being had a gift for stating the obvious in such a way it sounded an entirely new and brilliant idea.

The Great One, sitting on the throne in the center of the room, closed His eyes and drew a long, deep breath as if He smelled something sweet. This evoked the attention of the others who looked to

1

Him for an answer.

"Who shall we send?" asked the Great One. "Who will go for us?"

But the group knew even as He asked, the Great One had already selected His Chosen One.

"He has looked over the whole of the Greater Archipelagos," said the matter-of-fact creature.

"He has found one willing to go when comes the time," said the winged one.

"Who will aid in the decision that must be made by the people," said the last's counterpart.

The creature of the bronze skin stepped forward. "Whom have you chosen, Eternal One?"

The Great One stood from his throne to join the others, then crouched low over the transparent floor. He looked over the planet in question as it turned at His command amid the glittering stars. The others drew near and crouched as well, looking to where He would cast His eyes that they too might know the one He had chosen.

But as they encircled the planet, the Great One looked over the group, smiled confidingly and snapped His fingers that another planet in another realm would take its place in their view.

"You will choose one from another universe, Majestic One. Surely your ways are wondrous," said the factual creature.

As this one spoke, their view of the planet Kaern drew closer and closer until they could see one of their own, a creature of Paradise, standing before the door of a small cottage in a green wood. They watched as the winged creature spoke with the human woman at the door, who opened it wide for their comrade to enter.

"It is Viijelyk," said the being with the piercing eyes.

"He is already setting the wheels into motion," said the second.

When at last Viijelyk stood over the cradle of a two-month old baby girl, he laid a sword beside the child and vanished.

"This child is the one you have chosen," said the bronze being.

The Great One's smile drew the sweet fragrance of an innocent babe into the throne room. "Ivi," He said dreamily.

∞ I ∞

ERA

ERA SIGHED AS she peered at the clock for the tenth time in the last five minutes. This lecture was lasting far longer than was her preference, but most did. She preferred to be moving. Of course, listening to the same lecture she'd heard a hundred times by various instructors was technically doing something, but it made her restless even so.

Once every few months, the leadership of the hidden Isle of Atlantyss called the youth together to remind them of their purpose beneath the sea and of what was to be expected when the day came that their island would rise to the surface of the ocean and join the entirety of the Greater Archipelagos once again. The only details omitted were what it would really be like up above. She supposed those who had actually been there could not understand what it was like for those who'd been born after the island was concealed beneath water and had never been allowed to leave.

Era did know they had little to no technology on the surface. They didn't even have clocks such as the one whose face she kept wishing would tick faster. She knew, too, they had things she did not such as forests, sunshine and *swimming.* Though she had grown her whole life within the cover of water, protected by the sparkling transparent dome that kept the ocean out, she had never learned to swim. Most didn't, as swimming might encourage some to venture up to nearby islands, leading to Atlantyss' hiding place being discovered.

When she was young, Era had suffered from nightmares of Atlantyss' semi-transparent dome tearing and the city filling with water. She had since grown out of such dreams, but that didn't change the fact she was dying to get out of her bubble and explore the world above. When Iviana, the woman Era had heard prophesies about her entire life, had been reported to have arrived in the Greater Archipelagos, it had been an answer to prayer. If Iviana the Chosen One was alive in her lifetime, that meant she should be free from the cage of her city before she passed away, unlike many before her.

Her parents and teachers often reminded her how ungrateful she was in her longing to leave their great city—the favored island of the Great One—and she knew this was somewhat true. She loved nelepyres, running water and freedom to create (though she wasn't altogether creative). She appreciated clocks when they weren't moving too slowly, awakening to the glistening light of the clear dome over the city and the sea creatures swimming gracefully around it in colorful array. Her parents were understanding, loving people and she had a plethora of friends. But that did not change her heart's desire—her dream. She wanted to leap upon the back of a dragon and fly over the world.

Of course, if the least she wished to do was fly, there were always plenty of dragons within the dome, but she had never been brave enough to venture up to one. What if they didn't know any better and tried to take her outside the dome? Then there were the flying nelepyres, but nelepyres did not *breathe*. They weren't alive and wild. The wildness of the dragons was half her fear of them... but it was also what intrigued her, that and the fact they breathed fire. Still, even with such vessels as nelepyres at her disposal, she couldn't get far before hitting the dome and far was truthfully what she wanted.

Iviana was not only her ticket out of the ocean's depths, but her inspiration, her idol. She had heard the Chosen One was from another universe and had traveled to the Greater Archipelagos through an unguarded portal in the sky. This was done on the back of her own personal dragon who happened to be Tragor, the Great Dragon of the Ages, famous for his acts of power and bravery in the war against the dark dragons.

Iviana had visited Atlantyss some months ago and Era had been disappointed that not only had she missed out on meeting Iviana, she had not even known the Chosen One was there until after her departure, when she was reported to have simply disappeared before Era's best friends, Aedis and Merrick, who had been Iviana's guides. What she wouldn't have given to witness such a sight! Moreover, it would have been wonderful to meet the only other person on the planet who shared her Great Gift: seeking.

Era was discovered to be a Seeker at the age of five when her mother had lost her favorite heirloom, a necklace that had belonged to her great, great-grandmother. The moment the issue had been spoken of, Era had felt for the first time a fire burning in her veins and her feet began to move almost without her consent until she had discovered the necklace in a neighbor's home, stolen.

Things had changed for Era after that, at least for a few years. She remembered the way the city leaders used to watch her when she passed, the conversations her parents whispered in the evening when she could catch only a word or two. Then, of course, there was the day when it had been discussed she might have to be taken to the surface.

It seemed there was a shortage of Seekers in the realm and more than likely she was the only one. It also seemed Seekers were considered a prized commodity above and perhaps they should not have to be without one if it could be helped. Luckily, taking a child from the island under the sea and releasing her above was not only dangerous to their security, but was against the will of the Great One. That had been the day Era placed her unfailing love in the Great One Who had rescued her from being separated from family, friends and home.

The issue had not been breached again until a little over a year and a half ago, when their spies above had sent word the Greater Archipelagos was soon to be in need of a new Realm Leader and they were lacking a Seeker to locate one. She had come so very close to being taken to the surface that by that time she so longed to see. But then Iviana had been the Great One's answer when she was revealed a Seeker as well.

Era had hidden her disappointment well, but disappointed she had been. Though sending her may have been dangerous, she would have been relieved. She was fourteen and it was expected she decide upon her place within the city. But the only thing that interested her was becoming one of the spies who integrated themselves within the populace to gain information. Unfortunately, she could not qualify as a spy, for they were only selected from those thirty years of age or older—not to mention they were generally Swimmers, as it would be simpler to escape a difficult situation at any moment if one could breathe underwater.

Often, Era had asked why it was so important Atlantyss remain hidden. Of course, it was imperative no one mar the mysterious plan of the Great One, but some danger had often been alluded to. The historic texts read there was to be a time when the council above would become obsessed with power and control and the people would lack certain freedoms. That was why Atlantyss was kept hidden beneath the sea. But what happened to those who did not fall within the rules and guidelines—the approval—of that council?

Era sighed and checked the clock a final time before she heard the instructor utter the most glorious words in her vocabulary, "All excused."

ಌ2ೞ

IVIANA

THE TROTTING OF hooves sounded over the golden plain. Winter was just beginning to creep upon the bronze and scarlet of autumn, its frosty fingers making the ground sparkle. Crisp grass crunched beneath horses' feet as cold, misty breath escaped their lips and those of their riders.

Iviana sat upon a brilliant black stallion between two brown horses. Marquen and Darist were with her. The sight of them riding on either side reminded her of another journey, but that one had been a good deal longer and more painful, as well as enlightening and wondrous. This journey was to be short and... she could not decide what else, because, though she felt optimistic, she did not know their destination.

When she turned to ask Marquen, he smiled

reassuringly and that was enough. At least *he* knew where they were going. One could always count on Marquen.

Before long, they caught sight of a group of mourners clothed in ebony. The people looked to the three as they approached and a familiar young woman rushed to Iviana in tears. She was wailing something, but Iviana could not hear the words she spoke. Only the sound of her own heartbeat played in her ears as she saw the urn in the crying woman's arms.

The young woman took notice of what caught Iviana's attention. Opening the urn, she proceeded to spill the ashy remains into the frigid breeze.

"He's gone," she whispered.

"No, he's not," informed Iviana.

The ashes that had been carried away by the wind returned in black swirling tendrils, gathering themselves into the form of a man.

"Sorry, brother," spoke Iviana to the ashes, "we weren't done with you yet."

Next thing she knew, she was racing through the tunnels of the cannibal island, the cannibals right on her heels. Just as their grasping hands reached the skirt of her torn gown, the sound of arguing yanked her from slumber.

Iviana quickly sat up, grateful to be pulled from the familiar nightmare. It took her a moment to recall the reason she was sitting outside the back door of the council chamber, the one directly behind Flynn who sat in his marble chair on the other side.

The council was in session and though her usual impulse was to avoid anything that had to do with the council, she had made an exception to eavesdrop on this particular day. This day, they were to discuss the upcoming marriage of the Realm Leader.

Iviana couldn't help smiling as she recalled the evening Flynn had proposed to Brenna. It had been some time since they had returned from their journey in Kierelia, but Iviana had known since before their return what was to come between her friends. Flynn had surprised Brenna by asking for her hand in front of the whole of the island at banquet. Brenna had not been the only one surprised, however, for unbeknownst to Iviana prior, it seemed the council had expected to be asked their permission before the leader of the realm chose his bride.

This thought drew the smile from Iviana's face and replaced it with the rolling of her eyes. Even with Kurnin (a man whom Iviana detested for personal reasons) removed from their company, they were *still* the council. What had rather surprised Iviana was Flynn's willingness to submit to their discussing the issue before the engagement was officially sanctioned, as Brenna had replied with a gleeful assent herself. This had piqued Iviana's curiosity, thus her presence outside the door. She had not known, however, that they would be discussing a number of other far less interesting subjects before they came to the one that interested her. This had resulted in her unintended slumber.

Regrettably, Iviana realized they must have come to the matter while she'd been passed out, for Brenna's name was uttered a number of times before she had fully awoken to the remembrance of her reason for waiting there.

"I personally don't believe our Realm Leader could have chosen better," muttered one of the council who often traveled from another island to be present for the meetings. "She is of good, notable family and acts a lady in her own right, though she has shown tendencies to speak out when it was best she kept quiet. I think with a little tutelage from our council, she would be the finest companion for a Realm Leader in our history."

Flynn responded with, "No, Cinos, I don't want to change—"

"The point is, our Realm Leader ought to have given us *months* to look into the matter before the girl was even made aware of his intentions, let alone announce it before the island." This was from an older woman named Grandia, whom Iviana knew to be friends with Kurnin. It seemed Kurnin's influence was to plague the council whether he was in its ranks or not.

It was statements like the ones she was hearing that made her blood boil. How could Flynn *stand* it? *He is supposed to be Realm Leader and they talk over him as if he were a mere boy,* she thought. It seemed Flynn had grown in patience that was beyond her.

"I understand this has been the way of the council in past, but Brenna is by far an exception to such rules. She is kind, intelligent and unselfish and I think it our place to respect our Realm Leader in his choice." This came from Nimua's mother, Naii. The woman never failed to support Flynn in his difficult position.

There was a good deal of back and forth, but this statement changed the tone of the conversation that followed and by the end it had been agreed Flynn would have his bride. Iviana was not entirely pleased, however. She had wanted to hear Flynn put the council in their place, insist it was none of their business who he married. Still, their consent had spared much agitation.

Suddenly, the door Iviana was leaning against flew open and she found herself sprawled over the feet of her friend.

"Ivi?" Flynn stated, surprised. He bent to help her up.

"Hi," Iviana said with a smirk.

"You were eavesdropping? You shouldn't be doing that."

Flynn sounded more upset than she would have expected, but Iviana laughed at him. "As if I would go spilling the secrets of the council to the realm. Don't be such a worry wort, Flynn."

He relaxed. "Of course. I was just surprised to find you here. You don't usually take interest in the council."

"Well, this matter was different. I wanted to hear you defend your lady love. I must have been asleep during that part, though, because what I heard was utterly unromantic."

Flynn took his turn to laugh. "I usually just sit back until they've spoken their piece. The topic of conversation can change ten times in moments, but they eventually come to a conclusion about something when they get hungry enough."

"I believe it. I don't know how you manage, though. It would drive me mad sitting in there for hours every day."

Flynn shrugged. "Speaking of hungry, I'm starved."

"Lucky for you, I know a kitchen that's always open."

Flynn smiled a little sheepishly. "Thanks, but I've got to meet someone. I'll probably just grab a chunk of bread and run."

Iviana looked him over skeptically. "All right, Sir Mystery. I hope it's to tell your fiancé your wedding has been approved. I'm certain she's dying to know."

"Might be."

"Well, make certain you've told her before I see her or she'll hear it from me first."

Flynn laughed, but was obviously distracted with other things. "It's a race then," he replied and set off in another direction.

Iviana watched him until he was no longer in view. He had not been quite himself and she hoped everything was all right.

Sighing, she turned to race in the direction of her home where she had an appointment to meet a few friends for the noon meal. She knew she would be late, especially since she was supposed to have had a meal prepared by the time they arrived, but eavesdropping on the council had taken longer than expected.

It had been difficult to find Nimua with an hour of free time as of late. She seemed always to be busy with some small adventure with Necoli. But Iviana was simply glad he seemed to be fitting into their lives. She was surprised to find that, though the council obviously looked on the young man disapprovingly, they wholly ignored his presence on the island. She supposed his family was in better standing than hers, but couldn't entirely blame anyone for questioning him. He was certainly different from anyone in the Greater Archipelagos, refusing to dress in the garments of the realm, just as Iviana did most of the time. And he wore an earring, something the Greater Archipelagos thought gaudy for a man. Still, he was a truly pleasing person, as it happened, and had become a good friend, even if he had all but stolen her own friend away.

Still, she was delighted they were happy and she had Darist, after all. It used to be the three of them—Iviana, Darist and Nimua—on adventures together, so Darist, too, had all but lost what had been a lifelong friend. Even so, when they had spent time in Kierelia, he and Marquen had formed a strong bond, so the three of them often sat talking together in Marquen's cabin in the hills.

Upon their return, Marquen had gone back to his home in the mountains and proceeded to leave it rarely, the only exception to visit Iviana's own home. Still, he could no longer be considered a hermit now he had so many friends, thanks to the quest for the parchment. The group had grown very close during their travels and their bond had been sealed well by their encounter after Iviana had met the Anointed One, the son of the Great One.

Since then, they had attempted sharing their knowledge about the Anointed One, but it was received with a leery ear. The council, it seemed, scoffed at their story, according to Flynn, who had been made to take the brunt of it when he'd shared it with them. His being Realm leader meant they could not come out and call him a lunatic, but they had drawn as near as possible.

Having encountered such wonders that no one would believe was enough to make them feel distanced from the rest of the realm, as if they did not belong—even Darist, Nimua and Brenna, who had lived there their whole lives. Iviana had always felt this way, in truth, but it was no longer an option for her to return to her cottage in the FairGlenn wood, nor anywhere in the Kierelian kingdom. She had been amazed by how fast Sir Loric had spread the rumors of her using witchcraft and sent the promised hunters after her. She and her friends had barely escaped through the door in Jaela's Cavern.

She ached for the freedom to return to the home she had shared with her mentor, Naphtali, if only to gather those things that held sentiment. She hoped that, even though she was a wanted woman, her friend, Merri, would continue to send her eldest to look after her cow, though there was no one to tend the garden she and Naphtali has spent so many years on. Of course, for most her life, the people of FairGlenn had thought her a witch and, for all she knew, they still did. So, the wanted posters would be no surprise to them.

Whatever the case, she had left the little village on good terms when last she had been there, so she knew the one who had betrayed her to Sir Loric, calling her a witch, must have left the village before she had become an accepted and esteemed citizen. Often, she wondered if the villagers would protect her if she were to return but knew better than to hope for such a thing.

"Iviana, you are scandalously late!" cried Nimua as Iviana entered her hut. "Tell me it was because you were spending time with a new beau and I will let you off. Otherwise, you're in dire trouble for making me prepare the meal that was to have been your responsibility."

Iviana grimaced. "Unless you count the entire council, I'm afraid I'm apt to be punished."

Nimua turned to her with concern. "What did the council want with you? They weren't picking on you again, were they?"

"I'm sorry to admit I was only there to eavesdrop."

Nimua made a face that revealed her aversion. "Why would you want to do that?"

Iviana grinned confidingly and Nimua drew close. "I wanted to hear what would be discussed about Flynn and Brenna's engagement."

"I forgot about that! What did they decide?"

Iviana looked about, but the only person near was Necoli, who was setting the table on the patio. "Brenna isn't here yet?" she asked.

Nimua shook her head. "She said she would be late. Though how she could be later than you, I don't know."

"Well... they've approved the marriage—not

that they had any real say in the matter, in my opinion, but it should be clear sailing."

"Oh, I'm so glad. That council can stir up more drama than a war—not that I've ever seen one. Still, I've read of them. Anyway, I'm so pleased for them. Perhaps that's why Brenna's late. Maybe she's with Flynn."

"I think so. I was just with him and he didn't come out and say, but I can only assume—"

"But what if she *doesn't* know when she arrives? I want to tell her!"

Iviana looked at her skeptically. "We should probably let Flynn share it with her."

"Fine... but this is going to drive me crazy."

"Crazier than you already are?" asked Brenna as she suddenly appeared in the doorway. "What in the world could do that?"

Nimua threw a piece of bread at her. "None of your business."

Iviana laughed. "Come, lets eat. I'm famished."

While the four sat around the table on Iviana's patio, they discussed everything but what they were all thinking about. Brenna made attempts to breach the subject of the council meeting once or twice, but Iviana and Nimua quickly changed it to avoid temptation as it was clear Flynn had not yet told her after all. At last, to Iviana's relief, Leilyn, her old enemy, came waltzing up from the shoreline and monopolized the conversation.

"Are you discussing my wedding?" she asked. "I hope you know you're all invited. Even you, Iviana." She added the last as if it was a surprise even to her.

Iviana smirked. "I'm certain I'm grateful."

"But you *will* come?" asked Leilyn, almost demanding.

Iviana nodded. "Of course." Ever since Leilyn and Nico had finally set a wedding date, Leilyn had been impossible with wedding conversation, as if it was a planet-wide event.

"Oh, wonderful. But please, do wear some of our finer, local clothing and not that awful leather Kierelian garb."

"I shall aim to please," Iviana promised.

Leilyn then turned to Nimua and Brenna. "You two are my bridesmaids, as you know. I wonder, how do you feel about green frocks?"

Nimua shrugged. "It's fine with me. I'll wear whatever you want me to."

"And you'll each have your beaus to dance with at the celebration afterward." She returned her attention to Iviana. "But I suppose you'll have to sit

23

out the dancing." She shrugged. "Oh, well. It isn't my fault you won't give any of our local boys a chance. I *have* tried."

Iviana lifted her brows. "Woe is me."

"Though if you let me choose your garments for the wedding, you might just catch someone's eye and then you'll be able to have just as much fun as the rest of us."

Nimua grinned and could obviously take no more. "I suspect she'll take her chances. But, tell me, have you decided where the ceremony is to take place?"

"On the Grand Pavilion, of course. I've told you this."

"You don't want to select some place more memorable?" asked Brenna with concern. "Everyone marries on the pavilion and there are so many far more scenic places on the island."

"Then marry in one of them yourself," Leilyn retorted. "I want people to actually attend *mine* and they won't be able to if they can't find it."

"Touché," Necoli commented. He had grown to understand Leilyn well enough to know there was no winning with her; he simply wished to avoid another argument between her and the others.

"As if it's any of your business," Leilyn said with

24

a raised brow. "But then, I suppose it may be someday, if you'll ever pop the question to our Nimua. I do hope you have honorable intentions, Necoli."

Iviana could not suppress a giggle at his obviously flabbergasted reaction.

"Oh, just leave that to me," scolded Nimua, sending Iviana into another fit. She knew how Nimua detested Leilyn attempting to play the caring, pious friend when, truly, she could be a real pill.

Leilyn raised her arms in surrender. "Just trying to be helpful. Anyway," she turned to Brenna, "now that the council has approved your marriage, have you and Flynn had a chance to set a date?"

Iviana and Nimua gasped while Brenna's eyes went wide. "How do you know they've approved it?" she asked with a wide grin.

"Oh… my mother heard if from one or two of the council members. I didn't realize you weren't aware. I assumed Flynn would have told you by now." She said this more to the young women who sat looking at her with irritation than for Brenna's benefit.

"Does anyone know where Flynn is now?" Brenna asked as she stood

"Last I saw him, he was leaving the Council Hall

for some appointment," was the most Iviana could offer. "You could head that way and ask around."

With that, Brenna raced to locate her fiancé.

"Really, I wouldn't have spilled it had I known," Leilyn defended to those remaining. When they appeared doubtful, she added, "Truly, Brenna is my dearest friend. I know she would rather have heard it from Flynn."

Nimua relented at last and patted Leilyn's hand. "I believe you."

"Oh, but what a privilege to be married to the leader of the realm *and* to have the council approve it," said Leilyn dreamily. "If only it were me."

Necoli sat up and raised a brow. "We *were* just discussing your marriage to Nico, weren't we?"

Leilyn blushed. "Of course, but a girl can dream, can't she?"

Iviana chuckled, but Nimua scolded, "Certainly, but she shouldn't."

"As if either of *you* will be able to marry now, anyway. Well, I suppose maybe you, Nimua, but you're just lucky Necoli has fallen from grace right along with you."

"Excuse me?" asked Necoli. He was ordinarily a relaxed fellow, but it seemed he could take the jabs at his friends and himself no longer.

Leilyn held her hands up in defense. "It's not my fault. You're the ones who claimed the Great One had a son and Iviana had met this mysterious entity in person. I can't help it if every eligible man in the vicinity is going to think twice before courting Ivi. I've tried to help her, after all, but to no avail. She's sabotaged herself well this time."

Iviana and the others knew how true this was. There was no secret how people saw her. They thought her unbalanced, when putting it nicely, and assumed she had drug the others down with her.

Iviana knew the Anointed One had sent her back to the Greater Archipelagos for a purpose, but just what that was she could not say. She had thought it was to share his heart with his people, but those people were less than interested. In fact, Iviana had gone from being tolerated before the journey to something of a joke after. It seemed she was obviously as crazy as her father and grandfather before her and it was unfortunate she couldn't have turned out more like her great-grandfather, Latos. A Latos they could use right about now, as things were growing tense across the Greater Archipelagos.

Iviana and the others had yet to fully understand why this was, but they had felt it upon their return. They doubted even the people knew why they felt as they did, only that their spirits were picking up a sort of shifting in the atmosphere—a building up of something that was making it difficult to breathe. But as the Seers had nothing to say on the matter, it was wholly ignored.

Iviana described the feeling as the twisting and tightening of a coil—a coil that would eventually spring free, if they were lucky. Just who was doing the twisting was a mystery to her. The people? The council? The Great One or the Dark One? She knew no more than what she felt.

"Oh, by the way, Iviana," Leilyn said, pulling her from her revelry. "I was asked to let you know the council wishes you to attend their earliest meeting tomorrow."

Iviana weighed this, for if it was so, Flynn would have told her, wouldn't he? Besides, she'd been listening in. The only way they could have discussed it without her knowing was while she had been sleeping. "Who says?"

"No need to take that tone with me. It was Cinos. He caught me on my way here, asked if I would be seeing you and to let you know."

"But I just saw Flynn," Iviana retorted.

"So?"

Leilyn wasn't making it up, which meant Flynn

had neglected to tell her of this very important matter... and she had missed it during her nap. Pity. She had been so close to having foreknowledge of what was to come and yet so far. But she wasn't going to admit any of these things to Leilyn.

∞3∞

IVIANA

IVIANA STOOD UPON the steps of the Council Hall, gazing up at the tall structure and attempting to place its age. The years were apparent in the large cracks racing down the four columns as well as in the hole in which her foot was currently placed. She couldn't help wondering why nothing had been done to update what was presumably the most prestigious building in the world.

She had learned, some time ago, that the realm had at one time been under several small rulings until eventually it was split into two divisions, the East and West—each side secretly wishing to conquer the other. It wasn't until Latos, with his great anointing, charisma and servant's heart, had come into leadership that things began to change for the better. He had traveled to the western division where they miraculously agreed upon total unity, forsaking their own government to become a part of what Latos was doing for his own people, bringing order, unity and peace to islands that had been struggling with the opposite for so many years. It was why his reign had been called the Age of the Great One. The Great One had used Latos to bring harmony to a world that had for so long been in turmoil and it had come just in time, from the sounds of it. There was talk they might have entered into an all-out war if not for him.

Iviana wondered if there were other precious buildings such as this where the Realm Leader held council as he traversed the planet. As far as Iviana understood, Flynn was supposed to do that very thing quite soon. In fact, he was meant to have done so in the beginning of his reign, but he had forsaken it to follow Iviana on her quest, and a worthy quest it had turned out to be.

At last, Iviana realized she had avoided entering the Council Hall long enough and stepped up to the door. It was at once opened for her, revealing they had been watching her as she'd looked over the building. This was an awkward beginning for their conference.

"Thank you for appearing," said Cinos, almost

sardonically, revealing he had grown impatient.

Iviana casually sat upon the provided chair in the middle of the room—the part she hated most. "Oh, you're very welcome."

Cinos' expression conveyed his disapproval, but Iviana ignored him.

Instead, she turned to her friend. "What is this about, Flynn?"

"Admittedly, it is not I who has called you here," he replied, eyeing her closely to convey his meaning. "I must leave this matter to my council."

"Very well, then," said Grandia, the friend of Kurnin. "I'll take that as a call to the beginning of our meeting."

"Iviana of Kaern," began Grandia.

Iviana did not miss the suggestion she did not belong to their world in the mention of Kaern.

"We would like to speak with you about your previous journey."

"All right," Iviana urged, wishing they would not take so long in getting to the point.

"What was your purpose in taking your journey to the planet Kaern?" the woman probed.

As if they don't know. "It was not an outright plan. We were fleeing the cannibals you have now learned of and my Seeker's fire led me to a small portal I understand had not yet been discovered."

The woman nodded. "And how much do you know about the portals, Iviana?"

She shrugged. "Very little, really. I know you go through them to enter another world, either Kaern or the Greater Archipelagos. I would like to learn more, of course. I find them fascinating."

"Do you?" asked Cinos, stepping in. "Why is that?"

Iviana hesitated, getting the feeling she'd mentioned something she shouldn't. "I had not heard of anything like them before traveling to your world. They're somewhat... magical."

"You are not aware, then," began Grandia, "that portals do not simply appear from nowhere. They are placed, we believe, by the Great One. However, there was an Inventor, some time ago, who believed he had discovered the formula for creating portals. I do not suppose you have ever met that man?"

Iviana drew her eyebrows together. "Not to my knowledge."

"Are you absolutely certain? Keep in mind, this meeting is being recorded."

Iviana searched the room with confusion and two things became clear. First, there was not a single writing instrument moving in the room, which meant they had the means to record in some way she did not understand. Either that or there was someone hiding behind one of those big marble chairs. Secondly, they suspected her of some felonious activity.

"Can we cut to the chase?" Iviana asked at last.

"Very well, let us return to this in a moment," said a younger gentleman beside Cinos. "Iviana, we suspect you of an ulterior motive for drawing our Realm Leader from his duties for so long."

Iviana sat stock still, a cold chill waving through her. She had expected foolery... but not *this*. "Ulterior motive? Such as?"

Cinos halted the young man before he could respond and appeared to weigh his next words. "Malicious intent."

"*Malicious?* What more do I have to do to prove to you people I am not your enemy? Disapprove of me all you want, but do not accuse me of meaning this world harm. I consider the Greater Archipelagos home and want only the best for that home."

"Yet, within the first few days our Realm Leader took his position, you appeared to sweep him away from us when we needed him most. You were gone so long, we rather began to doubt you would return him to us."

"I told you I went of my own free will," Flynn broke in. "She didn't even want me to go—*I insisted.*"

Breathing hard, Iviana was grateful for her friend's intervention, but understood it was having no effect on the other council members, Realm Leader or no. Suddenly, she noticed an important member of this council was missing. It was likely the reason this conference was feeling so terribly one sided.

"Where is Naii?" she asked.

"Naii was unable to attend," said Grandia. "As Island Leader, she is a very busy woman."

Iviana watched as Flynn sat up at this, looking to where Naii should have been. Obviously, this was not something that occurred often, if ever.

"I will explain our quest to you once more and then I will leave you," said Iviana. "You may do with it what you will."

Cinos face grew red with irritation. "Iviana, I suggest you leave the course of this—"

Iviana cut him off. "You accuse me of malicious intent, so I will set you straight. I arrived in the Greater Archipelagos the day following Rhimesh's passing because I felt the same jolting loss you all did. Even so, the time I arrived was entirely in the hands of the Great Dragon, Tragor, who was the one who came for me.

"Upon arriving, I had no idea of leaving any time soon, but I was informed of Rhimesh's final wish and, forgive me, I followed through... with *your* approval. Flynn requested to join as, admittedly, I had my reservations about the quest and he meant to aid me in any way he could. I believe he felt it his duty, as much as mine, to fulfill the wishes of that wonderful woman.

"We traveled until we were hunted by the cannibals and then were led into Kierelia of Kaern where I, through a series of events, met with the very son of the Great One and learned he had given his life for mankind to save us from a dreadful fate. This is the story you were given upon our arrival and it is the one you'll receive forevermore.

"*And*, might I add, you ought to take greater heed of the message we were commissioned to find."

"The thing is," began the young man beside Cinos, who was obviously speaking against the older man's approval if Cinos' wide eyes conveyed anything, "the encounters you claim to have experienced were experienced by you *alone*." When

Flynn attempted to break in, the young man persisted, "We understand our Realm Leader has every faith in your claims, as do the others who were with you, but we cannot put *our* trust in their faith alone—people who are *your friends*. As it is, it rather appears as if our Realm Leader may not be able to see the situation without some bias."

Iviana's mouth dropped open, but she closed it as quickly as possible. This haughty young man deserved no dropping of her jaw.

"What he means to say is," began Cinos, "if you could supply some actual proof of your claims—"

"The book," Iviana reminded.

The man waved it off and finished, "—we might be able to overlook what appears to have been a plot formed by yourself and possibly others."

"You need *proof* to believe the message Rhimesh sent me to seek to understand how very perfectly good and kind the Great One is?"

"Now, now," began Cinos, "we have no desire to ruffle your delicate feelings. It is only that the claim our God has a *son* is rather more... sensational."

"If you would only read the book for yourselves," cried Iviana.

"A book written by whom?" he asked. "Entitled

37

what? It has no name nor does it name an author. We do not know from where or when that book came, only that it was already on your person before you left for your quest, which, might I add, makes the entire journey appear rather pointless, wouldn't you say? And that, I'm afraid, is where many of our doubts arise."

Iviana opened her mouth to speak, but Flynn suddenly burst with, "*Go...* Iviana. This interview is concluded." Iviana could see it had been nearly as difficult for him as it had for her. It was clear he had heard these things before. She only wished he had clued her in on them so she could have been better prepared. Why hadn't he told her what they were thinking? To spare her feelings? If so, he had only left her terribly vulnerable to their attacks.

"Very well, Flynn," said Cinos. "But Iviana, we must ask that you keep this interview to yourself. We prefer the matters spoken of in this room remain private."

Iviana nodded. Why would she want to go around telling people their highly respected council still believed her a menace to their world?

It was all Iviana could do not to slam the Council Hall doors behind her. They were large enough to shake the entire building, but she did not wish to give them anything more to hold over her. Not that she cared anymore of what they thought than she had before, but their thinking her a... well, a criminal could create actual complications for her life in the Greater Archipelagos. As she could not return to her home on Kaern thanks to Sir Loric, this was the only home she had left.

It was utterly discouraging to experience something like meeting the glorious, wonderful and warm son of the Great One and have it all thrown up in her face as hogwash when she attempted to reveal it to his own people.

Filled with rage, she tore branches from the trees she passed. She knew very well she might be observed in this enraged state by passersby, but could find no other outlet for the overload of emotion.

"*Delicate feelings*," she recalled from the mouth of Cinos.

At the memory, she picked up a large rock and made ready to fling it at a tree when a young child went running past. At the terror of nearly wounding an innocent bystander, not to mention a sweet-looking child, she glared down at her stone and dropped it. It was then she began to speak her burdens to the Ones whose business this really was, the Ones who had sent her, knowing she had no choice but to place her trust in them.

This helped her greatly and might have salvaged her mood had she not arrived home to discover her front door open. She knew very well she had closed it securely before leaving—not that anyone actually locked doors in this world, for they were a surprisingly trustworthy people. Even so, it was irresponsible to leave one's door unlatched, even if the back entrance was a gaping hole.

Pushing the door open, she expected to find one of her friends within and instead found a number of her cupboard doors ajar and her things scattered about. Moving into the bedroom, the trunk where she kept her most personal and precious belongings was pulled out and left open. Any papers it had contained were missing. She only happened to peer out at the patio to discover a number of these tossing about in the wind.

Racing to retrieve them, Iviana fumed over the fact her intruder had carelessly left the trunk open, but she realized the actual problem would be that they may have taken some of them and she would have no way of knowing. Not only that, but someone had actually broken into her home. Upon her return, she searched for clues as to who could have done such a thing, though she knew very well who had put them up to it. It had something to do with the situation from which she had just departed.

Glancing out the window, she spotted a figure on the beach. This was common, of course, for it was the best view on the island. The problem was, they were not enjoying the view. She was certain they had been peering her way. Of course, it might only have been the break-in playing with her mind, but she also knew it was perfectly possible her suspicions were correct.

She was being watched.

ℛ

Iviana was relieved when at last the banquet hour was upon her. She had spent the day putting her things in order, attempting to discover what, if anything, was missing. The thing was, nothing seemed to be. This being the case, what had they been looking for? Some proof she was conspiring against them, her every wicked maneuver written down where anyone could find it? She determined if ever she did take a turn for the worse and plot someone's demise, she would be much smarter than that. As it was, she had no such plans. All she currently desired was the relief of a full stomach and the comfort of her friends about her.

Arriving earlier than usual, she had reached the pavilion even before her friends—a first—and took the opportunity to select the most comfortable eating space. Leaning against a grandly large pillow, she rested her eyes until a shuffling of feet sounded beside her.

"Hey," said Nico, Leilyn's fiancé and the young man who had at one time pursued Iviana, as he took a seat beside her.

Iviana sat up, at once alert. Nico had not spoken to her for over a year after she had spurned his offer of love. What was he doing seeking her out now? Was he, perhaps, looking for some closure?

"Nico," she said, as if this was greeting enough. "Is there something I can do for you?"

"Oh, no, I just saw you sitting here alone and thought I'd join you. We haven't spoken in a while."

Iviana weighed this. "Yes, a long while."

"Too long."

Iviana raised her brows. "I suppose."

"How have you fared since your grand quest into Kierelia?"

"Oh... fine, I suppose."

"Good. Glad to hear it."

"You've been well I hope," offered Iviana.

"Of course. I am engaged after all."

Iviana smiled. "I whole-heartedly congratulate you."

Nico hesitated for a moment, then smoothed it over with, "That is kind of you."

As silence stretched between them, Iviana struggled to believe he was speaking to her without an ulterior motive. Perhaps he was attempting to make Leilyn jealous since she had been somewhat flirtatious with others over the duration of their engagement.

"You know, I never did learn why you led the others into Kierelia," he said at last.

The wheels in Iviana's mind turned with that statement. It seemed rather too like the lines the council had spouted. Recalling the times she had seen him recently, it seemed he might always have been with one council member or another. It was obvious he had grown rather chummy with them.

"The Great One," she answered bluntly. "That is all."

He nodded, obviously confused. "Why would the Great One lead you there if the answer was in that book you'd been carrying around?"

Iviana hesitated, uncertain whether placating

him would aid her situation. But she concluded she had no interest in it, replying bluntly, "I never told you about that book nor did I tell Leilyn."

"Oh, I think I heard it from Darist or someone."

Iviana thought this over. That was certainly a viable explanation. Still, she could not believe Nico's purpose in breaking their long silence his own.

"You are *exceptionally* early, Iviana," Leilyn accused as she sat beside Nico.

Iviana could not understand why her being early was worse than her own fiancé doing the same. Then again, this was Leilyn.

"You've *never* been this early, you know," Leilyn continued. "Were you meant to meet someone?"

Iviana stood then. This was more than she could take. Leilyn might be a pain, but the council using her to spy was too much. *Leilyn* being willing was too much, even if it was plausible.

"I've had enough," Iviana stated. "I'm certain I can find food enough at home. If it won't trouble you too much, tell the others I'll not be coming tonight." With that, she left them wide-eyed and open-mouthed.

Even so, just as she was clear of the banquet hall,

she heard someone stomping after her and was soon confronted by Leilyn.

"I want to know what's going on with you and the man I plan to marry!" she demanded.

"What?" Iviana could not tell if this was a clever cover-up or a misunderstanding. "Me and Nico? That was the first time we've spoken in over a year, Leilyn."

"Oh, of course, Iviana as miss innocent yet again, just like old times. You must know by now I'm smarter than that. I don't know how long this has been going on, but I *saw* him leaving your hut today, so you're already caught in a lie."

"Coming out of my house?" Iviana questioned. "Are you certain you saw the right one?"

"I think I know where you live. I'm not stupid."

"Leilyn, wait a moment. Around what time did you see him leaving my hut? Could it have been during the council meeting this morning?"

"Yes, it was early enough. You making him breakfast now? Trust me, you're not that good a cook."

"Leilyn... I was in that meeting with the council, remember? You're the one who told me I was to attend."

Leilyn's forehead wrinkled with confusion. "Then what was Nico doing in your hut?"

"That's what *I'd* like to know. When I returned home, I discovered someone had gone through all my things."

Leilyn appeared terribly bewildered. Obviously, this had not been what she'd expected. "Why would he do that?"

Iviana was uncertain she should reply, but wanted Leilyn off her back once and for all. "I think it had something to do with what the council spoke with me about. They... they're suspicious of me."

"Suspicious of *you*? You wouldn't hurt a fly."

Iviana laughed. "That's not what you said a moment ago."

"Well, it's easier to blame *you* than my fiancé..." Leilyn admitted with a meek smile. "Besides, I thought you'd been letting him woo you again."

"Can I just make it very clear I have never *ever* desired his attention."

This appeared to please Leilyn. "Well, and you have Darist now he and Nimua have split."

Iviana gasped. "*No*, I do not have Darist and never have had him, Leilyn."

"Fine, fine, have it your way. But look, if Nico

is letting that nuisance council tell him what to do, even so far as to invade the privacy of one of *my* friends, he's got another thing coming. I don't think you'll have to worry about him intruding anymore."

Iviana blinked back at her. "Why... thank you, Leilyn. I appreciate that."

"It's no big deal. I find he appreciates me more when I'm angry with him. Besides, I... consider you one of my good friends."

Iviana doubted Leilyn knew how to treat a friend if this was the case, but the words meant something to her anyway.

"Thanks, Leilyn. I'll see you around?"

"Or you can come back and eat if you like. I won't be a bother. And if Nico tries anything... I'll pinch him."

Iviana grinned at the thought, then sobered. "It's all right. I'm not in the mood anymore and... I've got some things to think over."

ଓଷ 4 ଓଷ

IVIANA

THE FOLLOWING MORNING, Iviana knew what she must do. It was imperative she see the one whose comfort was sure to ease her and whose confidence she could be absolutely certain. She made her way to the dragon's lair where she met a large, graceful creature whose piercing green eyes met her with adoration.

"Yes. This is what I needed," she said as she lay at his feet, ready to tell him of her troubles.

Gazing out over the green field where the other dragons congregated, her ease was shattered at the sight of a couple of teenage boys wandering near the edges of the valley. It wasn't as if she needed the valley to herself; it was only that she was aware of who those boys were and understood why they were there. She might have even doubted herself if they had not kept peering over to where she was. The fact that even Tragor seemed to understand what was happening as he glared back at them, his eye color deepening numerous shades, put a stamp on her suspicions.

"*Tragor...*" she sighed. "The council is questioning me again."

The large creature crouched low, inviting her onto his back, knowing the very thing she needed was to get away and *fly*. Iviana pulled herself up and fell into the crevices of his flesh as his great wings lifted them into the sky. The sheer rush of it had never worn off.

Suddenly, Tragor shot down, down, down and Iviana saw for whom he was aimed as the boys looked up and realized at the same moment, crouching low and uselessly shielding themselves with their arms. Just before Tragor might have done any number of things, he swooped over them and pointed his nose heavenward again, sending Iviana into a fit of giggles.

"If only I had you around when facing the council!" she cried.

But even the council vanished from her mind as the clouds enveloped them. Most days they flew together were spent exploring nearby islands. This day would be no different. Some time ago, Iviana had only visited less than a handful of islands, but thanks to Tragor, that number had more than tripled. Usually, they avoided the island inhabitants and explored the forests and mountains, but every now and then, someone would find her and she would enter their dwelling place for a meal and conversation. In fact, she now had several kind acquaintances on other islands, all of which no one on the Isle of Dragons was aware. She knew the council would not approve of her traipsing about freely without their permission.

Iviana often thought of one island in particular she wished to visit again: the "lost" Isle of Atlantyss. On her former quest, she had happened upon there hidden underwater city and discovered a whole secret society who served the Great One freely and passionately. Because of this, they flourished as a prosperous, technologically and mentally advanced people.

Long ago, the Great One had hidden them within a protective dome at the bottom of the sea that they would be set apart from the rest of the realm. It was prophesied that, one day, when the world was ready for them, they would be raised to the surface again and be used greatly for the advancement of the Greater Archipelagos. Iviana could only dream of such a day. She had loved their city immensely and the refreshing people had left an impact on her.

She had made a couple of young friends there by the names of Aedis and Merrick who were inventive geniuses. It was these two she missed the most, for though the three had spent only a few hours together, they had been kindred spirits.

It was at times such as these she recalled the acceptance she had felt there, craving it once more. She was glad she had Tragor that she could be free to explore and take her mind off what she was forced to await.

After hours in the sky of the beautifully tropical Greater Archipelagos, Tragor at last returned to the Isle of Dragons. Iviana took note of the way he flew in, perceiving he was attempting to conceal their arrival that Iviana might enjoy her privacy as long as possible.

Dropping her off on a secluded beach, she thanked him for the time they'd spent together as well as his thoughtfulness before he went on his way. Iviana sadly turned away, but cheered herself with the thought of food for her desperate stomach.

It was then she noticed for the first time an old

run-down shack near the beach. She began in that direction and was near the door when a low, crackly voice spoke to her.

"Do you know what the trouble is with becoming so old, passer?" muttered the stranger.

Iviana stopped herself in time to see the speaker of this statement who was, indeed, quite old and sitting on the ground against the wall of the shack. Upon closer inspection, his eyes could not seem to find her and Iviana realized he was blind. Peering down at his tiny legs, she thought they might possibly be crippled and could not help wondering if Healers could handle such ailments of old age.

"What is your difficulty, sir?" she asked.

"Eh..." The man offered a deeply wrinkled half-grin. "The trouble is nobody listens to a word you say when you grow as old as I. Think your head is full of bats, they do." He said this through a fine set of partially toothless gums.

Iviana drew closer. "What is it you wish to say? I will listen."

"Yes, I see that..." He appeared pleased with this, but soon his half-grin fell. "Eh... what was it I wanted to say, now?"

Iviana looked to the rising sun as her stomach growled.

"Aah... yes," the man said slowly. "Don't suppose you know our grand, young Realm Leader, do you, dearie?"

"I do," Iviana replied.

"Hear he's a handsome boy."

Iviana smiled. "So they say."

"Eh, but a handsome face doesn't mean a thing," said the man, his voice deeper than before. "It's what's in your heart what matters... and I grant you that boy's heart is as black as the rest of that fearful council, I do."

Iviana's smile faded. She was beginning to understand the bats theory. "No, sir, I know him personally. I assure you he is a man of honor and goodness."

The man raised his head as if he could see her face and said quickly, "What's that, you say? You know him personally? How so? You're just an ordinary girl, aren't you?"

"I was the one who brought him here in the first place," Iviana answered a little proudly.

To her astonishment, the man spat at her feet. "*S-seeker...*" he sputtered. "You're the Seeker?! I should have known the only person I'd get to listen to an old man was that fool Seeker," he said the last to himself a little hopelessly. He began to cough harshly then, evidence of an illness.

Iviana's compassion stirred and she knelt beside him, placing her hand on his back. "Sir, what ails you?"

"Go away from me! You're one of *them*. You'll have me locked away in the caves now, won't you? You'll have me shut away where no one—not even a fool Seeker—will hear me. This is a cursed land, girl, mark my words. We are a cursed people!" The man proceeded to wail and cough at once.

"Please, settle, sir. You're making yourself worse. No one is going to hurt you." Iviana touched her hand to his head and willed healing into the ailments of his body. The elderly man relaxed in response and fell into a deep, blessed sleep—a rest unlike he had had for some time, by the looks of him.

As Iviana sat cradling his head under her arm, she wondered why this man had not been healed previously; it had been too simple. She had not even used any curatives, yet as she searched his body with her gift, she knew the illness had fled at her touch. It had been a mere cold then, made worse by old age and neglect. Perhaps no one had known he was ill. It must be he lived alone in the tiny shack. She would have to ask if anyone could be made to come and take care of him. He was certainly too old to be on his own, so far from the dwellings of the villagers. If anything, *she* would come to him when she could. Nimua would know something about it. No piece of gossip got past her.

Iviana proceeded to slide the frail man onto a mat and drag him into the shack. So light was he, it was no time at all before she had him laid upon a shabby excuse for a bed. Before leaving him, she fluffed his pillow and covered him with a quilt, then prepared a meal with what odd bits she found in what might have been his kitchen. This she placed on the wooden crate beside his bed so he could enjoy it when he awoke. She would return to him when she could, but was uncertain when that would be. It depended on what she learned from Nimua.

☙

"Oh, old Waymith?" asked Nimua when Iviana described him. "He's still alive? I had no *idea*. I haven't heard anything about him for so long. Some years ago, he had been a council member, but there was an argument and he was made to give up his position. I don't know why he would be living in that old beach shack. He's got a perfectly fine plot of land further in. Come to think of it, I think that place is boarded up."

"What concerns me is that he was ill and may have been for some time. Does no one visit him? He is crippled, after all, as well as blind."

"Is he? How terrible. He wasn't before. It must have come on with age."

"And neglect. Doesn't the Greater Archipelagos take care of their elderly?"

"Well, yes, usually. But then, I suppose they usually have family to care for them and his only daughter disappeared years back."

This caught Iviana's interest. "Did she? Around the same time he was kicked off the council, I gather?"

"Mmm, I suppose it might have been near that time. I'm not sure. I was very young. I only remember it because of how furious my mother was about his removal."

"Then why hasn't your mother cared for him?"

"I really don't know, Ivi. Like I said, I thought he was dead. Maybe she did, too."

"Do you know where she is?"

"Visiting the Isle of Knowledge for a few days. A cousin of hers lives there, you know."

This frustrated Iviana, but it did not hinder her plans. Soon after leaving Nimua, she dashed to her hut and threw her kitchen pantry into a basket before heading for Waymith's shack. On the way, she gathered up an armful of richly fragrant flowers and brought them along, as well. If this man had been unattended as she suspected, he would need healing of the heart and spirit as well as of body.

It was nearly two hours after she had left him that she returned. Waymith was still sleeping peacefully in his bed, but she ventured to open the windows, allowing a fresh breeze to sweep out the dust and musty aroma of the place. The wood the shack was made from was very dark and the room was small, making it all the more cramped and gloomy, so she lit every scattered candle and lamp she could find and threw open the door.

She proceeded to toss out the sad little meal she had formerly prepared and began work on a filling one to replace it. She did not know if such an elderly man could eat the large array of food, but she meant to have it prepared anyway.

Then, of course, there was always the chance he would not even awaken until the following day. If he had been ill, he may not have been sleeping well and would need all the rest he could get. Still, she wanted to be ready and the food would be just as good the following day in any case.

Once that was underway, she found the curtains were torn and oppressive, so she pulled them down and did what she could to wash and mend them. Sometime she would make new ones, but these would have to do for now. Before she knew it, she was forced to sit and rest a few moments. She went outside and fetched one of the old, wooden crates beside the shack and carried it in to sit idly for a while

"Eh, who's there?" muttered the man. "If it's that vermin Kurn—"

"It's Ivi," she answered. "We were speaking before you fell asleep, if you remember."

Waymith sat up. "Ivi... We were talking? Oh, yes... *oh,* the *Seeker.*"

"That's right, but I mean you no harm, I promise. I wish only to ask some questions."

"Well, I won't be answering them," he replied severely before a great breeze blew through the small room and he caught scent of the wild island flowers and, more importantly, the food. "What's that I smell?" he asked gently, almost pleadingly.

"That's your dinner," replied Iviana as she fetched the tray and laid it in his lap. When she found he could not locate the correct utensils, she took them up herself and began feeding him.

The old man did not stop to think that a strange young woman was spoon-feeding him like a small child. He only gratefully accepted the offering and did not stop to speak until he had had his fill, which was, surprisingly, nearly the whole tray's worth.

As Iviana took the tray from his lap, he commented, "You're a good girl, aren't you?" It was not entirely a question, but there was a hint of speculation in his tone.

"I hope so," Iviana replied. "Now, how are you feeling?"

"My stomach feels as if it may deny all it's received. But I won't allow it."

Iviana held a cup of cool water to his lips, hoping it would help settle his stomach.

"Aah," the old man murmured happily as he lay back against the wall. "Haven't had fresh water for days."

"Oh!" exclaimed Iviana, reaching for the pitcher and filling his glass again.

"No, no, I couldn't take any more just now, but you set that on the box next to the bed and I'll get to it later. Now, what was it you wished to ask."

"Well, I... I wanted to know why you're living

out here all alone in this shack when you have a perfectly nice house near everyone else."

The old man seemed to peer at her a while, though he could not see, before answering. "That I cannot tell you."

Iviana was disappointed. She had so wanted to know that she might better help him.

"Got any other questions?"

Iviana nodded, then remembered he would not be able to see it. "Why were you removed from the council? And where is your daughter? Why is no one taking care of you?"

The old man's face was stern when she asked the first question, then softened and grew melancholy by the two that followed. He sighed, saying, "I cannot answer those either," as a tear dropped onto his cheek.

"But why not? I only want to help. I can't if I do not know more of your circumstances."

Waymith smiled. "You can't help beyond what you've done already. You ought not to have done even that."

Iviana shook her head. "I don't understand."

"I'm sure you don't and that's best. I suppose if you did, you wouldn't be here. Now, I'm tired, so you'll have to leave."

Iviana was again disappointed, especially at his change in tone. The softness had vanished, replaced with bitterness.

"Go now, please," he said impatiently. Iviana had gathered up her basket and moved toward the door when he added desperately, "Will you come back again some time?"

Iviana grinned. "Of course, I will. I'll see you tomorrow." Upon exiting, she returned to ask, "Do you like reading?"

"Sure, I like it enough, but I can't see a lick."

"I'll bring something to read to you, then."

❧

Iviana visited him the following day as well as every day for weeks, often multiple times a day. Each time she tried her questions, he denied her. Eventually, she stopped asking, for she could not bear the look that came over his face. Especially when she asked about his daughter. There was certainly deep heartache there.

It was days before she noticed the scars on his arms and legs when she attempted to wash him. He avoided questions over these as well. It seemed he would tell her nothing and so she must be content to know nothing and help him as best she could. Eventually, it became less about helping and more about the friendship that had developed between the two. Waymith was like the grandfather—even father—she'd never had, even if he was gruff and bitter at times.

When her friends began to notice her continued disappearance, she refused to offer even a hint of her whereabouts, considering it her duty to him. If he did not wish her to know anything of his circumstances, she doubted he would want her to share anything of their friendship.

What puzzled her was that when he refused to answer her questions, she got the impression he did so for her sake rather than his own. It was as if it was for her safety and he was determined to protect her. Often, he told her she should cease her visits, but always he asked if she would come again until he no longer needed to.

Sometimes, she would spend whole days with him, reading from her most precious book and telling him about her life. When she shared about her lonely childhood, he showed great compassion and understood her feelings, as he had clearly been disregarded and alone in his elderly state for who knew how long. How he had managed to remain fed, she did not know.

Once, when she came to see him, she heard voices within and knew she must not enter, must not even eavesdrop, though she dearly wished to. So, she hid herself and waited until she saw one of the council leaving the shack. When she entered, Waymith was paler than he had been for some time and was reeling with anger.

Iviana quickly knelt beside his bed and took his hands in hers. "Oh, what is the matter, my dear friend?" she cried.

The old man swatted her hands away and she withdrew to make up a plate of food for him.

"You can't come here anymore..." he said, "and I mean it this time."

"It doesn't matter. I'm not going to abandon you."

Waymith pounded on the wall with his fist and demanded she promise not to return. "They're noticing the food and the state of my health. They want to know who's doing it."

Iviana dropped what she was doing and sat beside him on the bed. "The council? Why should they care that someone is taking care of you? Why don't they want me here?"

The old man's face grew far paler and he began

to cough. "I shouldn't have told you that—I shouldn't have."

Iviana poured a glass of water and held it to his lips, but he would not accept it, nor would he settle.

"Go!" he commanded. *"Now,* or I'll hack myself to death!"

Iviana didn't know what to do, but recognized he was in no state to be quarreled with. "Fine, I'll go. I love you, dear friend." With that, she left him, but waited outside to be certain his coughing had ceased. Once satisfied, she headed for the Grand Pavilion to join the others for the evening banquet, something she had not attended for some time as she had been spending her suppers with Waymith.

Though Iviana was worried, she went calmly, knowing full well she did not intend to stay away forever. She knew he expected she would, that that was what her leaving this evening had meant to him, but she could not. She would return the following day, as she had done every day, and she would demand he tell her everything. He could not be expected to protect himself, crippled, blind and elderly as he was.

When she arrived at the banquet, her band of friends exclaimed how they had been missing her and were glad to have her with them again. Iviana tried to cheer for their sake, but was preoccupied with her own thoughts.

Brenna seemed distracted, as well, however, and Iviana could not help wondering about her. "What is troubling you?" she asked quietly.

Brenna looked around to be certain none of the others were paying attention. "I'm... worried about something."

"Do you wish to talk about it?"

Brenna thought a moment. "I do, but I don't know what you'll think of me."

Iviana was filled with compassion at the sound of her voice. It appeared Brenna had been keeping something inside for a while, but Iviana had been too distracted to notice. "Oh, please, share. I won't think poorly of you, I'm sure."

Brenna offered a half-smile, but appeared doubtful. "Well, you may, in any case, but I must speak with someone." She hesitated before, "You see, it... it has to do with Flynn."

"It's all right. Go on."

Tears pricked at the corners of Brenna's eyes, but then Nimua demanded their attention and charged into a grand story, so the two were forced to wait until they had another moment to speak. As it was, they found none, so Iviana offered to walk home with Brenna at the close of the meal.

"It's just that I'm worried about him," she said as they started. "He's been acting so strangely."

"How so?"

"Well... he hardly has time for me anymore. I realize he has so much on his shoulders, but even when we are together, he doesn't really talk."

"Doesn't talk?" Iviana queried. That didn't sound like Flynn. He loved to talk.

"That is, he does talk... a little. But I think something is bothering him. When things used to bother him, he would always come to me. He said it helped him. But now, he hardly tells me anything of substance. And... he's so distant. I think he's bored with me."

"He couldn't be bored with you!" Iviana comforted. "But I can believe perhaps something is going on with him. I'm sorry to say I have not noticed; I've been quite busy myself, lately."

"Ivi... I know you say you're busy... but I'm wondering if you could try talking to him... to see if maybe he'll tell you something of his troubles. I know he cares for you a lot and you've been friends longer than he and I have; you've been through more together... so he just might—"

"I doubt he'll tell me anything he wouldn't tell

you, but I can try."

Brenna was more relieved than Iviana had expected. "Oh, it would mean the world to me. I hate to admit it, but I've been doubting we should even be married. I mean, how can I be his wife if he won't share things with me? But perhaps a little urging from you will help draw him out."

Iviana doubted her speaking with him would help, even if he did reveal something. She could not be expected to smooth over issues in their relationship when they were married. That would likely only cause more trouble and would eventually cause Brenna to dislike her. Still, she was curious now and wished to see if what Brenna said was true, that he was struggling with something he had not yet shared with his friends.

ဃ 5 ෪

ERA

ANOTHER DAY OF classes were completed in time for the noon meal. Those who were especially gifted in certain areas ate a quick lunch before continuing for a few hours more. Though it wasn't necessarily a comfort to be ordinary, Era was glad she was not one of these, for she could only take sitting still for so long.

Once released, Era usually made her way over to the Kais building where she ate while her friends, Aedis and Merrick, worked. Today would be no different. In fact, she had been doing this for the past year since the two had been invited to become Junior Kais. At the time, she'd been upset she was losing her classes with them, but as, by that time, they had really only shared one class, she had rarely seen them anyway. Besides, she couldn't blame *anyone* for being willing to give up sitting around for lectures.

It was unusual the three were friends, for they had very little in common. Though Merrick was her own age, Aedis was a few years older, but this never seemed to bother the older girl. That was the reason Era looked up to her so much—that and the fact she was brilliant, as was Merrick. However, Merrick's ingenuity affected his social skills. This was why she and Aedis were the only friends he had near his own age. He got along best with the adult Kais.

Being neighbors, Era and Merrick had gotten to know one another early enough that his brilliance had not set them apart. There were, of course, those who teased him for being so different, but Atlantyss did not tolerate that sort of behavior, so Merrick was saved from anything that might have set him back. Instead, he was set free to become all he possibly could and, at the age of fourteen, that had gotten him to the position of Junior Kais. As far as Era knew, no one had ever been offered the position at such a young age. Though Aedis had been offered hers at the same time, she had been sixteen and even she had been young for the offer.

The Kais were a well honored group of ingenious and creative individuals who contributed much to their underwater society, so selecting young people to join them was no small matter. They were meant to impact their society in future and would take over as the older Kais retired or passed on. This gave the position a deal of grandeur in the eyes of the city.

When Merrick and Aedis had been placed in similar classes before joining the Kais, Era and Aedis had been introduced. Their relationship had begun with Era feeling a little over-awed by the older girl, but she eventually overcame it until the two were true friends. Aedis had become someone Era could go to about anything. And, since Merrick had formerly been her only best friend, it was pleasant to have a friend with whom she could share deep conversation. Merrick talked easily enough, but he was not comfortable with heavy conversation.

"Aaah, right on time," said Aedis as Era entered the room the two were working in. They were always happy to see her after classes let out, if not for her actual company, then for the meal she provided upon her arrival.

"I managed a fresh basket of honey rolls," Era said as she laid the array of food on the table. "And one of the Swimmers gathered a whole bunch of jujii this morning, so I grabbed two for each of us."

In addition, there was a finger salad of vegetables and nuts along with a plethora of other fruits and berries they managed to grow beneath the sea thanks to the light of the Great One's miraculous dome.

"I can't stop now," insisted Merrick as he worked on something utterly unrecognizable to Era.

Aedis dropped what she was doing and immediately took up her share of the jujii fruits. "I'll never understand why the gardeners don't grow these."

"It's too cool down here," Merrick mumbled over his work.

"You hush and finish up before these rolls get cold," Aedis demanded as she bit into one. "Thanks, Era. I haven't had a warm honey roll in weeks."

Era shrugged. "They're usually gone before I can get to them."

"Oh, I wasn't blaming you. It's not as if you *have* to bring us food. Of course, if you didn't we'd probably starve. You'd be amazed how easy it is to lose track of time in this building. Anyway, my mother doesn't do rolls. Says she can't get them to rise."

"Yeast," Merrick said.

"I guess hers always dies."

"Warmth."

"I thought I told you not to talk," Aedis scolded. Turning to Era, she said, "Anyway, how were your classes this morning?"

"Same," she said dryly. "I'll never understand your thirst for learning."

"Well, if everyone had the same attributes, life would be extremely dull."

"I suppose."

"Have you given any more thought about what you want to do when you've finished school—that is, if you choose to finish this year?"

"Of course I'm finishing this year. I'm not staying any longer than I have to and I'm not choosing a lifestyle that will cause me to have to."

"Well, what are you choosing?"

Era smirked. "I don't know."

"But don't you have to know by next year at the latest?"

"Exactly. I have a whole year. All I know is I want to get out and see the world. I think if I could get that out of my system I might have a better idea of what else interests me."

Aedis nodded. "But to get out, you have to be either a Swimmer or go undercover."

"Unless the Chosen One does her thing and we get raised from the ocean," Era reminded. "Then a whole world of possibilities will open up… literally."

Aedis' eyes lit up, for she loved speaking about Iviana, whom she, along with Merrick, was lucky enough to call a friend. "Yes, I suppose so."

"You two are so lucky; it is utterly unfair," Era said mournfully. "I still can't believe I was sick the day she came. I wish you could have brought her over."

"Well, we barely had time to do what we did. You know I would have if it had been—"

"I know, I know. Still, if only I'd been in classes that day, I might have caught a glimpse of her."

Merrick sighed as he took a seat, joining the two girls. "Honey rolls are cold."

"I told you," Aedis reminded.

"I know," he admitted. "Say, what happens when we really do have a world of possibilities open up to us? I wonder if we would leave the Kais to contribute elsewhere."

"You'd really leave Atlantyss, Merrick?" asked Era.

He shrugged. "Why not? You're not the only one who wants to see something of the outside."

"I've never heard you say so in all the times we've talked about it."

He shrugged again. "Things change when you

get older."

Aedis and Era smirked at one another over the table. Since Merrick had joined the Kais, he'd been big on the growing up thing. Era sometimes felt he saw himself as older than her. Truth was, he was only a boy at heart.

"Well, maybe we'll all do a little traveling, once we get the chance," said Aedis.

Merrick looked her over quizzically. "I thought you said you'd never leave Atlantyss, even when we're no longer submerged?"

Aedis laughed. "Well, I have moments of weakness, but you're probably right."

"Nothing is going to stop me," Era said dreamily.

"We know," Aedis said with a knowing smile.

"Boy, do we ever," added Merrick.

∞6∞

IVIANA

IVIANA'S FIRST THOUGHT upon waking was to visit Waymith, but recalling her promise to Brenna, she gathered up a picnic breakfast and started for Flynn's hut. She knew he would be there at that early hour, for the council did not usually meet until a couple hours before the noon meal. Until then, he usually stole what quiet time he could.

He was delighted to see her, mentioning how he had been feeling her absence from their usual schedule. As they conversed, Iviana watched for signs of what Brenna had mentioned, but could find no obvious difference in him.

"Flynn..." began Iviana with some hesitation. She did not want to bring Brenna's name into this, but she wished to know what could be causing her to worry to the point she was doubting their engagement. "I don't suppose there's anything you've been keeping from me?"

"Why on earth do you ask that?" he asked, surprised as well as a little perturbed.

"I don't know. I just wondered. We're the best of friends, but I expect you don't tell me *everything*. But if there was anything you thought you *should* share, that you needed to talk about..."

Flynn scratched his head as he continued signing the papers on his table. "Well," he began a little nervously, "I don't know if it's honorable to tell you at this point, but I feel I ought to get something off my chest."

"Of course, Flynn. Don't be bashful now," Iviana said with a mischievous half-smile. But this did not seem to ease him as she had hoped.

"Well, I... er." He looked up from his papers. "All right, don't take this the wrong way, but there was a time I rather thought I would be marrying *you...*"

Iviana raised her brows. "You wh—"

"*Don't* freak out. It was before you'd left for Kaern with Tragor—when you first brought me here. But then, of course, you left... and it didn't seem as if you planned to return. Brenna and I began talking and became good friends. Before I knew it, you were back, but I had already invested my feelings in her."

"Well, that certainly surprises me..." Iviana replied honestly. "I had no idea."

"That's good," he assured her. "I always wondered if maybe you might have shared my feelings. As my best friend, I wanted to be certain there wasn't anything we should put behind us."

"To tell you the truth, Flynn, I was pretty distracted with everything going on back then. I couldn't even say if I did or didn't care for you that way. But I know you are my good friend now and I'm happy for you and Brenna. Besides... I don't think the council would have allowed a wedding between *us* to slide."

Flynn laughed. "You may be right... not that I couldn't have handled them if I'd needed to. It's not like you're not worth fighting for."

"Oh, I don't think so. I know that council. I'm surprised you haven't found them to be too much for you as it is."

Flynn's smile dropped suddenly and Iviana regretted her statement. "I'm not saying you're not capable—"

"No, it's just... you're not far from the mark there."

"You mean you're having a hard time?"

Flynn's gaze stayed with her, but his mind was elsewhere. "Sorry," he said, snapping back. "Like you said, nothing I can't handle."

Iviana wished she could press him, but knew he would tell her in his own time if he needed. Besides, he had Brenna now and if they were to be married, she would need to shoulder the responsibilities of the realm along with him. Still, Iviana was certain he was keeping something from both of them. He suddenly looked so tired and it was true he didn't talk half as much as he used to. In truth, it occurred to her he *had* grown into rather a quiet person compared to the man she had first met. He listened readily to others, but it had become difficult to get him to share his feelings and opinions.

Now she looked him over as he dutifully worked through his paperwork, she was beginning to see the agelessness that came with being Realm Leader. There was a certain difficulty in identifying the age of his features, always shifting as Rhimesh's had, though not to her extreme; he had not been Realm Leader nearly as long as she. Still, it was faint, perhaps only a figment of her mind, but it would one day make him a fantastical creature. She hoped he would be prepared for it.

She needed to keep him in the forefront of her mind, speaking to the Great One about him daily. She knew *He* was aware of whatever was going on with him. He would see everything worked out as it should, even in Flynn's relationship with Brenna.

Flynn turned to her as if attempting to interrupt her thoughts. "Are you looking forward to Leilyn and Nico's wedding?"

"Wedding? Oh, yes. That's coming up, isn't it?"

Flynn chuckled. "It's tomorrow."

"No!" Iviana gasped. "I've been so busy, I had no idea."

"Well, *same here.* Good thing Leilyn pops in every day to remind me."

"You know she has a thing for you, right?"

"Of course. Why else would she bring me stone-hard rolls every day?"

Iviana laughed. "So long as you know."

"Don't suppose you're bringing anyone special with you?" he asked. "I guess it's the custom to do so."

Iviana's face brightened at his words and she stood to her feet, an idea sparking in her mind. "Actually... I am."

Abandoning Flynn, she raced to her hut to discover Necoli and Darist lounging in her kitchen.

"You've made yourselves at home, I see," she commented as she began rummaging through the cupboards.

"We came to see you, but you weren't here," Necoli stated. "Then, of course, you'd left some freshly baked bread on the table along with a pat of cream, so we, uh, helped ourselves."

"Well, I'm glad you did. Somebody's got to eat it. Though, if I could snatch those last few slices, I can bring them along."

The young men raised their brows at one another.

"Could you now?" asked Darist. "Picnicking with anyone special?"

Iviana grinned inwardly, fully aware of what they suspected. "As a matter of fact, I am."

Darist appeared surprised. "Who with?"

Iviana grinned widely. "It's a secret."

"A secret from *me?*" he asked with wide, innocent eyes.

Iviana laughed. "Yes, for now. But you shall see him tomorrow."

"So it's a *him*," Necoli said suspiciously.

"You're bringing him to the wedding, I gather?" Darist asked.

Iviana nodded. "I'll see you boys, then. Try not

to eat me out of house and home."

Heading out the door with her basket of food, she overheard Necoli bragging how correct he had been in his deduction as to why she had not been around as of late. This pleased her, for she knew what a marvelous jest it would be when she appeared with the man she had in mind for her wedding companion.

ଓ

Arriving at Waymith's shack, Iviana flew in with a cheerful spirit, greeting her elderly friend with a peck on the forehead and fully ignoring his angry expression until it transformed into a meek smile.

"I brought fresh bread again, since you said you liked it. I'm afraid some friends of mine got into most of it, but there are a few slices for you. Besides that, I hid away some jam so there's plenty of it."

"I told you not to return," said the old man humbly, pleased when she laid the plate on his lap and proceeded to pour him a cool glass of coconut milk.

"Yes, but old men have bats in their brains, you know. Or hadn't you heard?"

Waymith grinned. "Sounds familiar. What are

you so pleased about this day? Been meeting with a sweetheart?"

Iviana's eyes sparkled. "Something like that."

"I heard someone outside my window mention a wedding. I suppose you've got a beau to take you." He seemed pleased by the idea.

"Something like that," she repeated. She then offered him the glass of milk and knelt beside his bed. "I want *you* to come with me," she said. "I want to get you out of this lonely place and have you among people again. I even want you to move in with me, if you will, where I can take better care of you."

Waymith's eyes were stern at first, but were soon softened by her words. "You darling girl. You are so much like my daughter... Oh, I cannot go with you. You do not know what it would mean."

"I don't care what it would mean. You're done living this way. We've got to face whatever troubles you have and I am perfectly capable of doing so."

He shook his head vehemently. "It's too dangerous. There is much you do not know, child, and much I would not want you to know."

Iviana hesitated, then plunged. "Did the council banish your daughter from the Greater Archipelagos?"

Waymith's unseeing eyes grew cloudy. "They

did not."

"Then where did she go?"

Waymith was quiet a long while and tears streamed from his eyes, but he would not relent.

"I don't understand why you still can't trust me," she said.

He turned his face toward her through his tears. "Of course I trust you. I trusted you from the first meal you brought me. Problem is, I do not trust the others."

"There are few people I trust myself. We can live alone in my hut and you don't have to see anyone you do not wish to. You don't even have to tell me anything you don't care to. I won't press you. But you're coming with me tomorrow. As far as I know, most people think you're dead, so if everyone were to see you alive and well, nothing could happen to either of us. The council's hands would be tied."

The old man peered into the face he could not see for a while longer before he patted her hand. "All right, darling girl. I'll go with you."

"Truly?"

Old Waymith nodded. "Now, bring me all the food you've got. I want to gather what strength I can if I'm to escort such a lovely little girl to a wedding."

"You got it," she exclaimed merrily.

Before leaving, Waymith made her bend down to hug him and patted her cheek before shewing her, promising he would be as ready as he could when she came for him. Iviana promised him a fine jacket in return so he would look his best.

"Darist," Iviana began when she arrived at his hut the following day, "would you help me with something?"

He had just finished dressing for the wedding, but seemed in a rush. "Of course I will, but I'm supposed to meet Leilyn with the cake I baked for the wedding celebration. She wants to make certain it's acceptable."

"Well, it's a little late for that now, isn't it? She probably just wants to fit a little flirting in before the ceremony. I see Necoli coming this way. Can't we send him with it? He's nearly as handsome and twice as flirtatious as you."

"I suppose so," he said laughingly. "What is it you need my help with?"

Iviana rushed the cake out to Necoli with instructions to take it to Leilyn and give her a final thrill. She then took Darist by the hand and started for the beach.

"Are you going to tell me where we're going?" Darist asked a little breathlessly as she dragged him along.

"The beach."

"All right, and what do you need help with there?"

"We're fetching my companion for Leilyn's wedding."

"Oh... you, uh, need help with that?"

Iviana nodded. "I need you to carry him."

Darist choked, uncertain how to respond. Then he saw the old shack. "That's where he lives, I take it?" he asked doubtfully.

Iviana nodded with a grin.

"Can someone really live in that?"

Before he knew it, Iviana had raced ahead and entered the shack. Just as he approached, she came leaping out. "He's not here!" she cried. "Where on earth could he be? He said he'd be waiting."

"Perhaps he's already at the Grand Pavilion?" Darist attempted to help.

Iviana lit up. "Yes, perhaps he thought I was running too late and found someone to take him."

"Why does he need help getting there, Ivi?"

"He can't walk; he's crippled."

"Oh."

Iviana raced down the paths to the Grand Pavilion where the ceremony was to take place, but when they arrived, there was no sign of the elderly man.

"He's not here!" she cried, almost shrieking. Her stomach was beginning to knot.

As she was gaining attention from the other attendees, Darist pulled her aside to gain further information. " *Who is he?*"

"His name's Waymith."

"Old man Waymith?" he asked with both confusion and sudden understanding. "He's alive? How do you know him?"

"Oh, we met a while ago. It's who I've been spending my time with. He was supposed to come with me today. I can't imagine where he could be. It's not like he could go anywhere on his own."

Just then, the music that was to open the ceremony began and Darist worked hard to convince Iviana to sit down with him. Iviana's eyes scanned those in attendance in the hopes she had merely missed him. But when she was at last convinced of his absence, it was down to one question: What could have happened to him? Perhaps she should not have visited after he'd insisted she stay away.

Darist put an arm around her and did all he could to settle her, promising they would do what they could when the ceremony was complete. This helped some and, even in her trouble, she could not help noticing what a beautiful bride Leilyn made and how exultant she appeared when she saw Nico at the other end of the pavilion. Nico was more than proud when he caught sight of his bride and could not keep from grinning. It was apparent no amount of flirting with other men equaled what Leilyn felt for her groom.

Immediately following the ceremony, everyone began readying for the celebration. Iviana and Darist stole the moment to race back to the beach shack to discover what they could. Unfortunately, everything was as she had left it. Only Waymith was absent.

"Is there anyone else we can ask about this?" Darist suggested.

Iviana's mind raced. "I—I don't know. I suppose I could try Nimua. She was the one I talked to before and may have been more apt to notice anything."

Breathlessly, Iviana approached Nimua at the start of the wedding celebration, asking if she had heard anything.

"You're still seeing that old man? Why didn't

you tell me? I utterly forgot to mention him to my mother. Why don't we ask her?"

As the three caught sight of Naii, they proceeded to ask what she knew of Waymith, but her response was utter surprise and delight in the fact he was even alive. "You might try his old house," she suggested. "He may have returned there."

As the three turned away, Kurnin, whom she had not spoken with for some time, approached with a pleasant smirk on his large face, asking for a private word.

Darist and Nimua were loath to allow it, but Iviana assured them she could handle it.

"I could not help overhearing something of your search for old man Waymith," Kurnin started in once they were alone. "I wonder what your business could possibly be with him?"

Iviana froze, immediately sensing something amiss. "What business is it of yours?" she returned.

Kurnin's brows sprang up, but he pressed on. "I wonder, have you known him long? How long have you been caring for him?"

So he knew... or had guessed. Could he have had something to do with Waymith's disappearance?

"What have you done with him?" she demanded.

Kurnin's face filled with self-righteous indignation. "I cannot imagine what you could mean by that, young woman, but I resent your implication. The man has died, from what I hear. Passed away last night. I only wondered what your business might have been with him."

Iviana eyed him, testing what he had said with what she knew of him. Passed on last night? But why should Kurnin know anything about it? Whether or not his information was accurate, he was obviously attempting to pump her of information. She would give him nothing.

"I would ask my council, if I were you," he continued. "Surely, it is no longer a concern of mine, now I have been removed from leadership."

With that, he slipped away.

Iviana stood huffing, her eyes filling with tears. Oh, what was she to do? If he was truly dead, where might his body be? Somehow, she knew she must not ask the council about it. Kurnin's knowledge she had anything to do with Waymith was more than she wanted anyone to know and what Kurnin knew, the council would soon learn.

"Iviana, I'm so happy to see you here!" Leilyn cried warmly as she approached.

Iviana swiftly wiped the tears from her eyes and

put on her best smile. "You look absolutely stunning, Leilyn."

"As do you! I knew you'd be beautiful if only you tried a little. And I saw you came with Darist," she said with a knowing smile. "Just as I suspected!"

With that, she threw her arms around Iviana, giving her a good squeeze and went on her way to speak with the other guests. Though Leilyn would always be Leilyn, Iviana could not help being glad they were on good terms.

Even so, Iviana knew she would not be lingering for the remainder of the celebration. Now she had spoken with the bride, she considered herself free to depart.

"What was that about?" Darist asked as he approached.

"Oh... oh, Darist, Kurnin says Waymith passed away last night. I–I really don't know what to do."

Darist's eyes grew deeply compassionate. "Iviana... I'm so sorry. I didn't know the man, but I can see by your feelings his death is deserving of sorrow."

Iviana nodded, but her mind was elsewhere. She did not wish to admit to Darist she believed Kurnin was lying, mostly because there was nothing he could do about it, nothing anyone she trusted could do about it.

"I think I'm going to go home and lie down," she told him. She might not be able to sleep, but it would give her time to think.

"Of course. I don't blame you. Can I walk you?"

Iviana shook her head. "I'll be fine," she said with a small smile. "I promise."

Oh, Great One, please show me what to do.

‫ఴ 7 ఴ‬

IVIANA

IVIANA RACED THROUGH the endless tunnels in the mountains of the cannibal island. This time, she was aware she was dreaming, but the terror still kicked and breathed inside her. She assumed the cannibals were after her, but had no time to look back, knowing they would be right on her tale.

Suddenly, she heard the voice of a man who was as much a nightmare as the cannibals were to her. He taunted her and ripped at her nightgown, shredding it with his claws. When at last she allowed a glance behind, she found a giant version of Kurnin, putrid rot dripping from his mouth. Each time he tore at her hair and clothing, she cried with new panic. If Kurnin caught her, he would lock her away forever within the very heart of this mountain, she knew it.

But why should she think he would lock her

away? He seemed rather more intent on destroying her. Still, the deeper she ran, the more certain she was her race would lead to her imprisonment. Even so, she could not turn back, for Kurnin was always behind her, ever pressing her forward.

Soon, she could hear voices crying far down the corridor, warning her to turn back or join them in their fate. For they had all been imprisoned by Kurnin, just as he wished to do to her now.

But learning this, Iviana no longer feared for herself. Instead, she worried about what she would find at the end of her pursuit. The thought of others being locked away set a fire *blazing* in her that would not subside until she had freed them. The closer she drew, the hotter she grew until her own skin felt as if it was melting off.

At last, she entered a huge room with high ceilings carved within the rocky mountain, but what drew her were the bars that ran from ceiling to floor on three sides of the room. Behind the bars, were people, hundreds of them, each with heartbroken spirit. She drew near to a woman who looked on her with compassion, as if certain Iviana would join them there.

"Why are you imprisoned here?" Iviana asked her.

"It is the secret law of our land—the law only the highest members of leadership are aware of."

"But what law has you held here?"

Horror filled the woman's eyes as Kurnin suddenly had hold of Iviana and was attempting to eat of her flesh as if he was a cannibal of the island. The woman in the cell cried for her to get away and stay away, else this would be her fate. "Wake up!" she cried. "You must awaken!"

Iviana bolted upright in bed, sweat dripping from her skin, pouring into the fresh scratches on her arms and legs, making them sting. Even her nightgown was torn and tattered. But stronger than anything was her Seeker's fire, ablaze and burning within.

Recalling her visit to the Isle of Atlantyss, she thought over the class on dream interpretation, attempting to sort out the meaning of this nightmare. But it seemed too deep for what she had learned in the lecture. It was as if she had literally been inside the mountain, pursued by Kurnin's spirit or a like spirit. Furthermore, she knew she had truly spoken with the woman and it was she who had awoken Iviana before the spirit could devour her.

Iviana was uncertain of what to do. Could there truly be a prison within those mountains? If so, would the cannibals not have consumed their prisoners already? But even as she wondered these things, she stood and dressed herself, for she would follow the leading of the Seeker's fire into that mountain and discover what was at its heart. Cannibals or no, it did not matter. Fully awake, she did not fear facing them again. She would best them, if she must.

The hue of the night sky proved it was only midnight and she was grateful. She had no intention of notifying anyone of her purpose. They would think her unbalanced for following such a dream, not to mention what they would make of her tattered arms. It would look as if she had been attacked, though attacked she had been in a way she did not understand. It was as if in her race through the mountain she had faded between dream and reality, spirit and flesh.

It did not take long for her to take to the air with Tragor, who had been alerted to her need of him by the Great One and had been waiting not far from her hut. She now understood why the dragon was always there when she needed him, for she knew the Great One better now she knew His son and it was They Who provided for her every need.

The pair flew for hours before reaching the

island, but it was yet dark enough to conceal her from the eyes of the cannibals whom she had allowed to haunt her dreams for far too long. It was ridiculous to let anything take up residence in her life in such a way, awake or dreaming.

When she drew up to the entrance in the mountain where a large boulder had guarded it, the great rock was already drawn aside, as if prepared for her arrival. She could only hope it would remain so when and if she was ready to depart.

Once within the tunnel system, she followed the fire in her veins until she came to a place where she recalled having felt the Seeker's fire the last time she had been there with Necoli—when first she had discovered the island and had been forced to rescue her friends from the cannibals. In that moment, she had ignored the feeling as only a passing fancy. Now, it was time to discover what her spirit had perceived that day. She had never truly forgotten it, for it tugged at her consciousness just as the cannibals had persisted on dwelling in her dreams.

Her blood turned cold as she heard the sound of hundreds of breathing people, but everything in her grew numb when she stepped into the room of her nightmare. In truth, she had not really expected to find it—had not wanted it to be true. Whatever was happening here was like the death of the Anointed One: unjust. The desire for justice replaced the burning of the Seeker's fire, causing her vision to glow scarlet for a moment.

"Why have you come?" asked the woman Iviana had spoken with in her dream only hours before, her question birthed of anguish rather than curiosity.

"How do you know me?" asked Iviana. She wanted to be certain the woman had truly spoken into her dream.

"You were here not long ago," she said. "I warned you not to come."

"I don't understand how you know what I dreamed—how you were able to communicate with me."

"You were not truly dreaming, though sleeping you were. You were... dream-walking. I can see things in the spirit realm that others cannot. For instance, you are surrounded by a blinding brilliance that keeps the daemons in these mountains from attacking or attaching to you. It sears the spirit realm like a flaming sword."

Iviana nodded, though she hadn't a clue what the woman was speaking of. Still, it was nice to know. "Why are you here?" She looked about at all the people within the prison. Many of them ignored her, too oppressed to care. Hope gleamed in the eyes of a few others. Some were so wan and pale she was certain they had not seen the light of day for years upon years. All were on the brink of starvation.

A middle-aged couple drew up to the bars before Iviana. "You look familiar," said the woman.

Iviana studied the couple thoroughly. "I'm afraid I don't know who you are," she admitted.

The woman's perplexed expression did not fade, but she said, "I see. I am Shynn and this is my husband Japha. The woman you've been speaking with is Jaela."

"Jaela? As in—"

"The cavern," Shynn supplied. "She is of Jaela's direct lineage, a granddaughter, if you will. Who, may we ask, are you?"

"I am Iviana."

"How have you discovered this place? You are not of the island."

"No, I am not. I dreamed of you this evening and followed my Seeker's fire."

"Then the Great One has shown you. This could mean—"

"Don't, Shynn," said her husband. "It's no use and not worth this girl's life."

"You must go, Iviana," urged Jaela. "You must tell no one you have found us."

Iviana crossed her arms. "Not before I understand what this is about."

Jaela released a huff of breath, as if giving up, but Shynn supplied, "This is where they keep the... uniquely gifted... those with Great Gifts deemed dangerous to the realm."

"Dangerous how? The Great Gifts are anointed by the Great One. They are not a danger."

"That depends on your interpretation of danger," said Japha.

"The council is greedy with power and they fear anything that could prove more powerful than they," explained Shynn. "Not all share this reason, however. Some are simply uncomfortable with certain gifts. They are ill at ease with anything outside their interpretation of the Great One's ways. But their closed-mindedness combined with power has made them an enemy to those whom the Great One loves."

Iviana grew ill. The council had known about the cannibal island long before she and her friends had found it. Flynn had said he was handling it, but he must not know what secrets the council held. She was not certain of them herself. "The council has imprisoned you here. You have yet to tell me *why*."

"It was begun by Kurnin," said the voice of an elderly man not far away. His voice made Iviana's stomach tighten. "When he was first instated as Island Leader of the capital island and placed on the council, he won many council members to his side, as well as some outside the council."

Tears began to fall from Iviana's eyes, for she knew the one who spoke to her. It was Waymith.

He continued, "When this island was first discovered to be inhabited by cannibals, it should have been brought to justice and its people saved from their horrific practices. Instead, Kurnin saw it as an opportunity. In exchange for the council's silence and allowing them to continue living as they wished, the cannibals agreed to keep this prison within their labyrinth. They are the ones who keep us fed—"

"Barely," Japha added.

"And clothed."

Japha rolled his eyes.

"Waymith," Iviana whispered through her tears.

It was then Japha realized Iviana knew the elderly man and helped him forward.

When he was set upon the ground before her, Iviana reached her arms through the bars and took hold of his hands. Tears flowed freely down her face.

"It is my fault you are here, isn't it?" she said. "They imprisoned you here because I was helping you. They wanted to leave you for dead and I got in the way."

"No, no," cried Waymith. "I demanded they take me here. I did not want them to discover who had been nursing me to health. I had to get myself out of the way so you would be safe."

Iviana only sobbed harder. It truly was her fault. She had pressed him too far, had tried too hard to take things into her own hands.

"This is the girl you told me about," Jaela realized, kneeling down beside Waymith.

"There, there, dearie," Waymith comforted. "It is not so bad. *Your* courage only gave *me* the courage to do what I ought to have done long ago. It brought me to my daughter."

Iviana looked up and saw the arm Jaela had placed around Waymith... her father.

"This is what happened to your daughter?"

Waymith nodded. "I may tell you now what I would not before, for it is clearly too late to conceal it from you."

"Father, let me," said Jaela. "You are too weak."

Waymith nodded and Jaela began, "Years ago,

back when my father was on the council, Kurnin was forming his pact with the cannibals and developing his secret brotherhood. It was his goal to imprison those whom he deemed dangerous… that included me. When my father learned of their plans, they tried desperately to win him to their side. When they could not, they beat him daily, until he became what he is today. When he was too old, beaten and sickly, they left him in that shack to fend for himself and hid me away here.

"From what he tells me, a few members of the council brought him food from time to time. For years, they did just enough to keep him alive, but nothing to heal his wounds or his crippled legs—the legs they themselves had crippled with abuse and neglect. It was months before you discovered him that they had stopped seeing him altogether, had stopped keeping him alive, for he was meant to have died long ago. I believe it was only the Great One's grace that kept him safe, that we could be together again." She looked on her father with a teary smile and Waymith patted the hand she had placed on his back.

Shynn continued with, "My husband and I were not imprisoned for our gifts, like most. We were simple Healers. Unfortunately, we not only discovered the cannibals, but also the prison. We then made the mistake of attempting to inform the council of our findings. We were immediately returned and locked away with the others.

"Jaela, here, is one who was imprisoned for her gifts. Her Seer's eye is not only far more accurate than is natural, but she possesses seven other gifts, half of which had never been seen before. Over there," she pointed to a sad, young blonde girl, "is Teena. She can read the thoughts of others. Retra, beside her, is a Shifter. Byron," she pointed to an older man not far from them, "can *fly*. Nemlin can move things with his mind…" And on she went.

Iviana could only shake her head. Her world had just turned upside down. Certainly, she had always disliked the council—especially Kurnin. She knew they could be *irritating*, but this corruption was beyond anything she had ever known. She began to understand why Marquen had seen fit to hide himself in his hills, why the council had hated her for not only having a gift, but having multiple gifts. She could scarcely believe she had not been imprisoned. The fact she was well known as the only Seeker may have been the only reason she had been spared.

Shynn stopped her introduction of the prisoners. "My dear, are you all right?"

Breathing hard, she replied, "No. Of course not. This is unjust... this is—"

"We should not have told her these things," said Jaela.

Iviana turned to her. "But why not?"

Jaela only shook her head.

"Jaela fears what you will tell others," said Shynn. "She fears for your life. She has been here from the beginning and has seen too many join her fate."

Iviana's heart went out to Jaela and to every prisoner, but there was something they did not know. "I see no way that I can get you out of here on my own, but there is a new Realm Leader. He was not raised in the Greater Archipelagos and we are very close. He will save you all from this injustice."

"No!" cried Waymith, reaching for Iviana's hands through the bars. His eyes filled with passionate tears. "You must trust *no one*, do you hear me? You do not know this land like we do. Jaela's own mother was on that council with me and had Jaela placed here *herself.* You don't think we trusted her with our whole heart? Promise me you will flee this prison and tell no one what you have seen. It may even be too late, if you're found

escaping. You must be careful, my sweet girl."

Iviana wrenched her hands away from him. "I can make no such promise! I promise only to return to you, either as a prisoner or to free you—*all* of you." With that, she fled the dark, somber room.

Jaela and Waymith's pleading followed until she was out of sight, but Iviana cared not. She was sickened. She hated that this realm, that so prided itself on unity and purity, had secretly stooped to such a level, that an entire realm had allowed it to happen, knowingly or unknowingly, by letting their council do what they would at will. *She* would not. But how could she fight it?

☙

Iviana tapped lightly on the door to Flynn's hut. She knew he was probably still sleeping, for it was yet early, but hoped he would awaken to the light tapping. She did not wish to alert others to her presence at his doorstep in the middle of the night. She had dealt with enough rumors in the past.

Thankfully, she heard a shuffling within the structure before a weary Flynn, with hair in a tumble, pulled open the door with a yawn. "Ivi, what are you—"

"Hush. Can I come in?"

"Of course." He stepped aside to welcome her.

Iviana lit the lantern on the table. "Sit down, Flynn."

He did not hear her, staring instead at the wounds on her neck and arms. "*Iviana*, what happened?" He turned from her, saying he would find some ointment a Healer had left with him for a cut. He returned with a warm, wet towel and began patting at her wounds.

Iviana attempted to swat him away. "Never mind that, Flynn. It's a long story and it's not why I'm here. Flynn... there's something you don't know about the council."

The towel in his hand paused as he peered up at her. "There is?"

Iviana couldn't help noticing the waver in his voice, as if he was frightened, but could not fathom the reason for his reaction.

"I went back to the cannibal island."

Flynn's face was a mess of worry. "Why in the world did you go *there,* you crazy dragon-lady? And all alone! No wonder you're so beaten. For goodness' sake, Iviana, what got into you? I told you I was handling it."

"That's just it. You're not handling it, because

you can't. There's something you don't know about that island... and you're really not going to like it."

Flynn's eyes dropped to the table, but not before they had betrayed him.

Iviana's stomach dropped as well, but she would not believe what she had seen. Watching him closely, she continued, "There's a secret in the heart of the labyrinth."

Flynn's gaze did not leave the table and his face was beginning to pale.

Iviana found it difficult to breathe. *"You know?"* she cried, her eyes sparkling with sudden tears. "How could you not tell me? I've been asking and asking about that island. Why has nothing been done? Kurnin and his *'brotherhood'* should be imprisoned."

Flynn's eyes met hers at last. Seeing tears there, he grasped at her hands. "Don't be upset, Ivi. I only learned of it when we returned from the Great One's quest. When I told them about our run-in with the cannibals, I assure you I was shocked by their lack of surprise and it was quite some time before I got them to confess their secret. I've been discussing it with them ever since, trying to form some compromise. I just haven't been able to get anywhere with them."

Iviana's mouth fell open and the tears dried with

the sudden heat of her cheeks. The pounding in her heart was all she could hear for a few moments before she drew her hands from his. "*Compromise...?*"

Flynn's tone grew desperate as he said, "I know it sounds pathetic; trust me. You just don't know these people. They're wily—dangerous. You have to be careful how you tread. I've been dealing with them this way for months. It's all so much more difficult because I went with you on that quest. You were right when you said I shouldn't leave. Kurnin got his claws back into the council while I was away and stirred up a lot of trouble for me. It was all Naii could do to hold my place. It seems Kurnin started some secret brotherhood before he was ousted from the council, but the brotherhood did not die with his position. I've had to kowtow from the moment we returned from the quest just to keep things in order, to keep them from dismissing me."

Iviana's heart softened. She knew well how Kurnin could be and there was no way she could understand how difficult Flynn's position was. She had never tried to govern an entire planet... nor anything else for that matter. "There is a courageous man inside you that I know and love well. Being stuck in that stuffy room with that stuffy council day after day has stifled him. You've just got to unleash him on that wretched brotherhood, for the sake of those people."

Flynn appeared frustrated, thinking over her words, but swiftly frustration turned to anger and he leaped from his chair to pace the room, fuming with thoughts Iviana could not read. "This all started in the name of *your* great-grandfather, you know," he said bitterly.

"Oh, did it?" Iviana scoffed. "Pray, explain."

"They did it because they feared losing all that Latos did for the realm in bringing it into peace and order."

"I'm sure that's what they *say* and maybe it's even what they think, but *come on*, Flynn. You're not a boy anymore; you're a leader chosen by the Great One. *Lead them*. I mean, if you made use of the gift He gave you, you could have this world turned upside down."

Flynn's eyes flashed as he spat, "You think I can just go around using my gift to control people? You have no idea how careful I have to be, Ivi." He took a breath, settling himself. "I'm dangerous," he finally admitted, looking wearier than she had ever seen him. "Being a Speaker isn't a *gift*. It's... it's more than I know what to do with. I mean, you remember when my sister was ill?"

Iviana nodded.

"When I spoke out my doubts, she grew worse again. If you had not stopped me, my words could have *killed* her. I could have killed my own sister and not even known what I was doing. I don't know the full extent of what I could do... the damage that could be wreaked."

He paused and took a deep breath while Iviana studied his anguished face. She could feel the fear emanating from him. She realized now why he had grown so quiet of late and wished she had known sooner all that he was thinking about his gift. She could have been helping him with it, testing its limits, discerning what circumstances warranted its use.

"Besides," he continued wearily, "the council obviously does not care much for gifts such as mine. If they thought I was using my words to turn their minds to my will, I would end up in that dungeon as well, if not dead.

"As for those prisoners," he added. "...not everyone on the council is as messed up as Kurnin. It cannot be that many of the people in that dungeon do not deserve to be there."

Iviana's blood turned cold at his words. Looking

him over a long while and at last turning away, she pressed her eyes closed, for she understood something she wished she did not. The man behind her was a stranger. She understood the transformation Brenna had been seeing. Flynn *had* compromised and he was one of *them* now.

‮ఴ‬8‮ఴ‬

IVIANA

WITH NAII IN TOW, Iviana climbed the stairs of the council hall. After leaving Flynn's hut, she had raced to Naii and Nimua's home. To her surprise, they had already been up and dressed. It seemed Nimua had been alerted in a vision that Iviana was in some distress.

Iviana spared no time in telling them all she had discovered. Naii had been shocked and ashamed she had unconsciously let her fellow council members keep such a secret from her. Had she known, she could have done something sooner. It was all her traveling to other islands that had made it possible to keep such secrets.

It was difficult to convince Nimua that Flynn would be no help to them. She simply could not believe he had strayed so far from the friend they knew. Iviana understood, for she would not have believed it if she had not seen the puzzle pieces fall into place. Of course, he looked worn and weary with shadows under his eyes. It was a wonder he could sleep at all. Though Flynn had sounded callous toward the plight of the imprisoned people, he would surely be struggling with guilt. It would have been months since he had learned the council's secret, judging by how long he had not been himself. It wasn't a wonder he had felt so far away, keeping such a secret from them. Who knew what else he was privy to that he had not shared.

The three had discussed what could possibly be done. Iviana knew no way of freeing them from the prison without a key, for the bars that held them were wide and strong, obviously made to last for ages. In addition, they would need someone to contain the cannibals while they moved the people out of the mountain and off the island. Actually getting them off the island was the main complication, however, for they would need numerous dragons and Swimmers for such a task. Homes would need to be found for them, as well. Not to mention the work that would need to be done in healing the people physically, mentally and spiritually after such a horrific experience.

There was simply nothing to be done but to confront the council and reveal to the world the injustices that had occurred. Hopefully, the world would be on her side.

The look on Flynn's anguished face when he caught sight of Iviana's entrance into the council chamber was a blend of guilt, irritation and... terror. The latter two ripped through Iviana's heart. Though she had spent hours convincing Nimua he would not help them, she had not truly believed it until that moment. That was not the look of one who was prepared to support her.

"What is this young woman doing here, Naii?" called Grandia. "We had nothing scheduled with her."

Naii gazed over the whole of the room, including Flynn, searing them with her blazing lavender eyes. "She has something she would like to discuss."

Though most of the room was left momentarily speechless by her icy glare, Grandia replied, "That is all very well for her, but she is not a member of this council and does not decide when she will make an appearance. She may put in a request and we will look into her matter."

"I am one of this council," declared Naii, "last I

checked, anyway. And I make her welcome here today."

"Oh, very well," said Cinos impatiently. "Lets get this over with."

"*No*," called the fearful voice of the young Realm Leader. All eyes turned to him, but he offered no explanation, only stared into the floor.

Iviana knew he was frightened. Of what, precisely, she was uncertain. But before anyone could back him, Iviana began, "I want the prisoners freed."

Flynn shot her a miserable glance before returning his gaze to the floor.

"Excuse me, young woman?" muttered Cinos as if she was crazy.

"The prisoners you have held captive within the mountain on the cannibal island—I want them freed."

Long ago, when Iviana had first faced this council, they had been all murmurs and shouting. This time, they were silent. Iviana hoped that was a good sign.

Tentatively, Grandia asked, "You have seen for yourself what it is you speak of, I imagine? This is not some rumor?"

Iviana glared at the woman. "I know as well as

you that it is there... and birthed of this council... Kurnin's 'brotherhood.'"

"Iviana, do you realize what a serious accusation you've just made?" asked another gentleman of the council. He turned on Naii. "I suppose you believe this girl's lies?"

Naii's face grew deep red with anger as she glared back at the man.

"Oh, *come on*," interrupted Iviana. "I did not come here to beat around the bush or watch you sidestep the issue. You have committed a serious transgression and every person who is or has been involved will have to answer to the Great One. No one has the right to determine His anointed gifts are unsafe or—"

"Blasphemous," said Grandia. "Blasphemous is what they are. Those people's gifts are not of the Great One. They are given by the Dark One himself to wreak havoc on this world."

"Here, here," said another gentleman.

The murmuring and shouting of old commenced and Iviana did not attempt to gain their attention. Even so, a loud whistle sounded through the room and all eyes turned to its source: Naii.

"What have you to possibly say for yourselves?!" she demanded. "You have kept this from me for a reason and it is the conviction in your hearts that knows it is wrong."

"No, Naii, it was that we knew you were not to be trusted," replied a woman to the right of Flynn.

"Why have you not told the world what you have done, if not for your shame?" cried Iviana.

The room fell silent again.

"Flynn," Iviana said softly, longingly. "What have you to say?"

Flynn returned her gaze, but his thoughts were no more readable than before. He did not reply.

"Flynn?" she repeated with meaning. She could not give up on him—not yet. Her Flynn was in there, somewhere.

"The boy is wise beyond his years," said Cinos. "He saw the light in our argument long ago—he knows the truth. He will not be turned by a mere Seeker, granddaughter of Latos or no. You forget, young woman, how you entered our world: against our laws. You have shown no respect for our land since then. You fled us the first chance you got. Why should you care about the affairs of the Greater Archipelagos now if not for some ulterior motive? If not to take the place of our Realm Leader yourself?"

Despite such a heavy accusation, Iviana paid him no mind. She continued looking to Flynn. Waiting.

When the room had grown uncomfortably quiet for all but Iviana and Naii, Grandia spoke in a closing tone, "I think that is enough for today. Iviana, we will discuss your view on the matter tomorrow and let you know, personally, what we come up with. Before you go, however, we need you to sign—"

Iviana did not remain to hear what the woman would say. She fled. Not entirely certain why she did so, she knew it was for more than one reason. Firstly, she had the feeling she needed to get out before they forced her to sign some asinine agreement. Secondly, Flynn. Flynn's behavior had been too much for her.

Before she had gotten far, a strong hand pulled her from the path and behind a row of bushes.

"*Ouuch!*" she cried as she recognized who it was. "Could you pull any harder, Flynn?"

"What in the world did you think you were doing in there?" he shouted. "What did you think you were going to accomplish?"

Iviana could not believe *he* was irritated with *her*. "What were *you* doing in there? You just sat there!"

"Ivi." Flynn rubbed the back of his neck until it grew red. "You've just sentenced yourself."

"*Sentenced* myself? I assume you're going to stand by and watch that happen too."

"I'm not kidding. You have to go... now, *today.* You have no idea how hard I've had to work since Rhimesh passed to keep you safe. Those people... *do not like you.* Kurnin *hates* the very sound of your name. If you don't go, you're going to get yourself killed... along with the rest of the people in that prison."

Iviana's mind reeled. She could not care less what happened to her, but she cared about those people, about Waymith. But was the council truly capable of going that far? She supposed Flynn knew better than she by now.

"You can't tell anyone else what you saw. It's the only chance those people have."

"Why?"

"Don't you see? If the rest of the realm learns what you have, the council will have to cover it up before it's exposed... if it's not too late already."

"Then lets go—*now!* Lets go and get them out!"

"How do you propose we do that, then?"

Her mind raced. She couldn't save them. Especially not if she was dead. A deep hatred rose within her chest, for herself, the council, for Flynn. Oh, especially Flynn. Flynn had betrayed her. He was Realm Leader. She would not believe there was nothing he could do. Problem was, he was too afraid, too tied up in the dirty games of the council and Kurnin's insipid brotherhood.

"I'm leaving," she said angrily, on the verge of numbness.

"Where will you go. You're a wanted woman in Kierelia, remember?"

Iviana glared at him. "You're the one who said I had to go. There's nowhere else *to* go. I'm going *home*." Iviana rushed away from him, uncertain what she would do to him if she remained. Besides, from the sounds of it, she needed to get out and quickly.

Upon reaching her hut, Naii and Nimua were waiting for her.

"Iviana, you must leave," said Naii.

"I know," she said bitterly. "Flynn just told me."

"I'm sorry. I really thought once they had been confronted, they would relent. Instead, I'm afraid it has put you in terrible danger."

"Well, what about you?" asked Iviana as she stuffed her travel bag with the few things she truly cared about.

"I am the leader of this island and, thankfully, I am well-loved. I am not easily gotten rid of. But

Nimua must go with you."

"What?" cried Nimua. "I'm not leaving you! They aren't even aware I know."

"You are my daughter and Iviana's best friend. They will assume, and rightly." She turned to Iviana and gripped her wrist. "Take her, will you?"

Iviana stared back into her eyes. "I don't know that I want to leave you either. Won't you come with us?"

Naii shook her head. "I am Island Leader. I will not leave my people. I'll be fine."

It was difficult for Iviana to relent, but she knew it was not her choice. "All right." She turned to Nimua with, "Come with me?"

Nimua was yet unconvinced as Naii faced her. "Please, Nim. Do this for me?"

Nimua glared back at her mother until her face softened. "Fine."

"Good." She reached under Iviana's table and drew out Nimua's bag. "I packed this for you."

Nimua looked as if she would cry.

"Can we come in?" called Darist from the patio.

Iviana was surprised to see Marquen there, as well, away from his cabin in the hills. "What are you doing here?"

Darist watched as Iviana rushed about to put her

things in order. "What's going on?" Turning to Marquen, he asked, "Is this why we came here?"

"Oh, Darist, I'm glad you're here," said Naii. "Where's Necoli? I asked him to meet us here. Oh, no matter, you're here. Listen, Iviana and Nimua are leaving for Kierelia. I was wondering if you would mind coming with me to escort them to the dragon's lair in case of any trouble."

"Not at all," he replied, utterly bewildered. "But why are they leaving... so quickly?"

Naii shook her head. "They are in danger. We cannot tell you why or it will endanger you as well."

Darist shook his head. "Danger in the Greater Archipelagos? Oh... the council." He thought a moment. "I'll return as quickly as I can."

"Where are you going?" cried Nimua.

"To pack. I'm coming with you."

Iviana shook her head, but grinned at Naii and Nimua. Of course loyal Darist would come without even an explanation.

"I, uh, already have my bag," said Marquen.

Iviana blinked at him, understanding the Great One must have shown him something. "All right," was all she had time for as she prepared to leave her hut for who knew how long? But even as she did this, a thought occurred to her. "Dragons won't do, will they?" she asked Naii. "I don't like to have that many dragons in Kierelia. It would draw too much attention and put them in danger."

Naii thought a moment. "You're right. It will have to be Jaela's Cavern."

Finally, Necoli arrived, already packed. Nimua ran to him and he pulled her into his arms.

"You're coming with us?" Nimua asked, relieved.

"Of course," he replied with a smile. "I'm not letting my best girl leave the universe without me."

Iviana was satisfied to see this news ease her friend as she darted into the kitchen. Their group had grown and so must their supplies. Most likely Darist would think to pack whatever he could spare and, between them, it would have to be enough. She felt an urgency in her blood, as if something was horribly wrong, even more than she was already aware of.

"You all right?" asked Darist as he returned and began helping her stuff food into their bags. She noticed he had an over-sized sack full of food with him.

"Something is wrong."

"No kidding? I wish I knew what."

"No, more than that... we have to hurry."

Naii overheard and gestured for the rest to join them in the kitchen. "You're all here," she said with some relief, "Once you've finished in here, you must go."

"Where are you all going?" asked Brenna as she entered the hut, her eyes wide with confusion.

Iviana looked her over and realized she had been crying.

"What's wrong, Brenna?" she asked as she rushed to her side.

"Oh, I thought you would be alone. I just wanted to talk."

"What is it? It's all right, we're all friends here."

"Well, I've just broken off my engagement with Flynn."

"You did? Why?"

But Iviana knew why.

"We got into an argument. He said some terrible things. Something is wrong and I wanted him to talk to me about it. Of course, he wouldn't. He never does anymore. And I just had to... to end it. I can't marry him."

Iviana hugged her friend tightly as Brenna cried into her shoulder, but Naii touched her back to remind her they must go. "Oh, Brenna, I know how hard that must have been." *And what a day Flynn must be having.* "Oh, but we simply must go. I cannot tell you why, but if you would like to join us, you're welcome. However, I warn you, I cannot promise your return."

Brenna looked up in surprise. "Is something the matter? Does this have to do with Flynn?"

Iviana nodded. "But telling you would put you at risk."

"I see," said Brenna, looking a little shocked. "I wish I could say I'm coming with you, but my mother is ill and I must stay for her."

Iviana regretted leaving her behind at such a time, but knew that even though Leilyn was Leilyn, the two were very close. Leilyn would be there for her. "I understand. We'll miss you and... take care of yourself."

Brenna smiled and brushed the tears from her face. "I hope all is well with you. Be safe. I love you, dear friends."

Suddenly, a pang similar to her Seeker's fire rushed through Iviana's body, revealing it was imminent they leave immediately, so she gave Brenna and Naii one last embrace and gestured for the others to follow.

ℭℨ

As the group made their way to the door into Kierelia, they started toward the dragon's lair, where, thankfully, Tragor was at that very moment. Iviana ran ahead of the others that she could have a moment to say goodbye. As she embraced him, she prayed it would not be a forever farewell. She could not bear never seeing him again, but had no way of knowing where all this was leading them. When she pulled back, his eyes bored into hers. It seemed he did not understand her at all, which was not a common occurrence.

Iviana quickly filled him in on the details of her situation and the reason she could not bring him along. Knowing he was a very old dragon and must be very wise in his years, she knew he accepted all she had told him. Then, as the others caught up to her, she threw her arms around him once more. Tragor watched as she disappeared and her heart felt as if it would split in two.

It wasn't long before they came to a large cliff-face with a blood red door wedged into the rock. She faintly recalled that door from the other side; it was mostly identical on this end. She had never passed through it before and wondered if it would be anything like the portal in the sky she was accustomed to.

All of a sudden, Iviana heard Nimua gasp as the sound of a great number of people came charging toward them, as if they would yet capture Iviana, if not her friends as well, who would now be considered liabilities. As it happened, Iviana and her friends were much closer to the door than they, so the race began.

Iviana was the first to reach it and as her hand grasped the dragon-faced handle, she wondered if it would open for her. It had rejected her once before. If it did so again, she thought she might lose it. Thankfully, the door swung open, almost as if pushed by some force on the other side, and a shifting opalescent substance shimmered before her. It almost reminded her of the dome that covered the Isle of Atlantyss, but she had no time for a true comparison as she was pushed through by the others. In much shorter time than it took to travel through her usual portal, she was on the other side, standing within Jaela's Cavern.

Once the others had tumbled through, the door closed behind them and Darist held the handle still in an effort to keep their pursuers from following.

"Darist, it's no use," she called as she started through the tunnel, the others following.

"Besides," Nimua said breathlessly, "I highly doubt there will be many—if any—who would venture through that door. Most are too afraid of this world. I'd venture to say we may not even need to hurry."

"That's a thought," added Marquen. "Likely, they'll have Flynn add us to the list of those unable to use the door."

Necoli nodded. "I'll venture to agree, and thankfully. This is too much running for me. What do you say we slow it down, Ivi girl?"

Iviana's mind raced. Could they chance it? Running wasn't going to be possible for much longer, anyway, as the tunnel was about to grow more cramped. Besides, they needed to conserve their energy.

"All right," she gasped. "My side aches anyway."

"Thank the Great One," puffed Necoli. "I've been living the easy life too long."

ഇ9ൽ

ERA

ERA AWOKE WITH a start. Breathlessly she pulled the covers back and found her body scratched, her nightgown torn and shredded. How had this happened? Next thing she knew, she was standing outside her body, looking down upon it. But whose room could this be? She did not know it. And, wait... the body on the bed was not hers at all, but that of another woman.

Somehow, she understood this woman with the beaten body to be that of the only other Seeker in the realm, Iviana of Kaern, the Chosen One. Era could not understand how she had ended up in what was likely Iviana's bedroom, but as she could not turn her head away from the Chosen One, she realized she must be dreaming.

Suddenly, Era was no longer in the bedroom but

soaring through the sky beside Iviana where she sat upon the Great Dragon of the Ages. Had she not already been aware she was dreaming, she would have been terrified, for it truly felt as if she was soaring through the winds, just as the dragons did. She journeyed beside the two until they landed on an island she had never seen before. Then again, she knew none but one—her own.

Iviana made her way through the island until she came to a passage in a mountain. Through it, Era followed her. By this time, she seemed to have formed a link with Iviana's emotions and felt all that Iviana did: determination, confusion, dread. Era wished she knew why they were feeling as they did, what their purpose could be that they would travel through this labyrinth with such resolve. Where was Iviana going and why was she being drawn along with her?

She did not have to wonder for long. Soon, Era could hear the breathing and murmuring of what must have been dozens of people. Before she knew it, they had entered a large cavern containing hundreds of people caged behind bars that reached from ceiling to floor.

What in the world could this place be?

Iviana raced to speak with some of the people

held prisoner there and Era quickly followed, not wishing to miss a thing. As Iviana received an explanation for the prison, Era listened intently, memorizing every word spoken and letting it sink into her heart. As she eavesdropped, she began to realize what she was experiencing was no mere dream; it was a vision of a real occurrence. For whatever reason, she was witnessing this scene for a purpose and she must remember it well.

Suddenly, Iviana pulled away from the people she had been speaking with and fled the place. Era attempted to follow, as she could not be certain where she was and would not know the way back to... No, Iviana could not help her. She must awaken...

Era awoke with a start. Breathlessly, she pulled back the covers, absently checking to see that she was in her right body, in the right bed and the correct room, with no harm to her body or bedclothes. She released a relieved sigh to find all was as it should be.

Yet, it wasn't, for she had witnessed something she shouldn't have in the natural realm. Question was, what was she supposed to do about it? Luckily, there were no lectures to be held this day, so she had all day to sort it out. Firstly, she would speak with her parents.

Dressing quickly in order to meet them for the morning meal, she raced into the kitchen to find her mother and father eating quietly at the dining table.

"Are you all right?" her mother asked.

Era realized she was breathless and gulped a few breaths of air down. Taking a seat, she accepted the plate her father offered, though she did not feel capable of eating it.

"I had a dream," she said.

"A nightmare?" her father asked.

"I thought you had moved on from your flood dreams?" said her mother.

"It wasn't another flood dream, Mother. I saw the Chosen One."

"Well, that's a nice change. I'm sure that was pleasant."

"It didn't feel like an ordinary dream. I followed her and I could feel what she felt. She found this prison in a mountain where innocent people were being kept in some sort of dungeon for those blessed with unique gifts."

"All right, not so very pleasant," her mother admitted.

"Sounds like an odd one," said her father. "That seems to be all the dreams I have, random. The other night, I dreamed I was on board a large vessel that both floated on water and flew through the sky. It was certainly thrilling. Felt as if I was really there."

Era shook her head. "I felt the same way, Father, but this was different. I think it really *did* happen."

Her parents exchanged glances.

"What makes you think that?" asked Father.

Era thought a moment. She couldn't exactly explain just why. She simply knew. "It was as if I was being shown for a reason, so I could help or something. Perhaps the Chosen One needs me."

Era's mother looked her over. "Why don't you talk to that dream class instructor about it. Perhaps your dream has some symbolic meaning."

Era nodded. She didn't like this response; she wanted her parents to take her word for it. She knew the dream was not a symbolic vision. She even began to wonder if she had experienced a sort of transport.

C3

A while later, she met Aedis in the Kais building. Aedis was busy working on some project, as always, but never turned Era away when she needed her.

"You look a little pale," said Aedis when Era

entered. "Did you sleep all right?"

Era shook her head. "I'm not altogether certain I did sleep."

"Oh?"

"You see, I had a dream..."

"Well, that means you slept, doesn't it?"

"All right, I suppose I slept, but I want to talk to you about the dream I had. It was about the Chosen One."

Aedis' eyes lit up. "It was a good dream, then."

"Not really. I started in her bedroom where she had just awoken. It appeared as if she had been beaten, though she was obviously surprised by the sight of her wounds."

Aedis raised an eyebrow. "How odd. Go on."

"Well, next thing I knew, we were flying to some faraway island. It was on that island I followed her into a mountain where there was a large prison for people with extra special Great Gifts. It was supposed to protect the realm from them, from what I gathered. I overheard her entire conversation with a group of the prisoners and the whole thing is really horrible. I must find a way to help somehow."

"But it was only a dream."

"That's just it; I don't believe it was only a dream. I believe I was seeing something that actually happened."

Aedis studied her friend and Era hoped it was because she believed her.

"Perhaps you could try talking to the dreams lecturer about it."

Era was disappointed by the doubtful tone of her voice. "That's what my mother suggested," she said unhappily.

"It's not that I don't believe you," said Aedis, reading her thoughts. "But it *is* hard to believe. I would simply like to know what Cadence has to say about it."

Era sighed. "I suppose I should try speaking to her."

"Oh, Mikal," Aedis called to someone who was passing by the door. "Would you mind sending for Cadence?"

Immediately, the young man left on his errand.

"You can send people out like that?" Era asked, impressed.

"It comes along with the title of Kais—even if you're only a Junior Kais. I don't often use it, but I would like to hear what she thinks. You don't mind, do you?"

Era shrugged. "Why not?" *What could it hurt?*

But when the woman arrived and Era explained

the experience, Cadence only shook her head and said it was too detailed to be given a meaning just then, that she would have to pray about it. Era agreed to this, hoping the Great One would defend her case.

Just then, a group of Kais were heard passing through the hallway, loudly discussing some matter. Era shrugged it off, for she rarely understood the Kais' conversations, but Aedis' attention was captured as she made her way to the door.

"What's wrong?" she asked them.

If Aedis was concerned, something important had to be taking place, so Era drew herself up behind Aedis to listen in.

"The Chosen One has fled the realm, it seems," one of the Kais replied gravely.

Era leaped out from around Aedis to face the group of adults. "How come?"

The man shrugged dejectedly. "We are uncertain, but she was seen by one of ours' fleeing the people of the Isle of Dragons. She escaped through the door to Jaela's Cavern with a handful of her companions. The reason is not yet revealed at this time... other than that she is rumored to be an enemy of the planet."

"I wonder what could have happened," Aedis

said with concern.

"An answer would be nice. But the real trouble is, we are uncertain of how she will return, for it is further rumored the Realm Leader will key the door to deny them."

"Can't one of ours' change it?" Aedis asked.

He shook his head. "Only the Realm Leader's blood is allowed access to the controls."

"So what does this make of the prophecies?" someone asked.

A grave, even fearful, silence passed through the group, but the Kais who had spoken formerly said, "The prophecies are the word of the Great One. We must trust that all that is to be will take place in His timing. It seems they will simply not come to pass in the timeline we expected."

Era stepped away, deep in thought. If her dream really had been more than a dream, she was fairly certain she knew why Iviana had been chased from the realm. And with her gone, what were they to do about those imprisoned? Era didn't even know the actual location, as she knew little of the world above, having never been there. If she could only get someone to listen to her, she might be able to do something herself.

And she determined she would, if possible. She

could not help feeling betrayed by Iviana the Glory-bringer knowing she had actually abandoned them—not only those imprisoned, but the entire realm, the realm that needed her and the island beneath the sea that counted on her.

ಏ10ೞ

IVIANA

IVIANA HAD FORGOTTEN about the hundreds of spiders and their sticky silver webs that awaited at the end of the tunnel and was met with a mouthful as she stepped through. Before she had time to warn the others, Nimua and Darist began to squeal as they were enrobed in the spiders' thick, dusty silk, sending Iviana into a fit of laughter as she raced from the cave.

"You dreadful girl!" Nimua cried, hurriedly wiping the layers of webbing from herself. "Why didn't you warn us?"

"I have to agree with that outburst!" exclaimed Darist as he did the same.

"You'd think they'd never seen a spider before," Necoli said laughingly. "I, for one, have been in far worse scrapes."

"Oh, I can't blame them," Iviana relented. "I forgot about the spiders and was nearly as shocked myself."

"Well, where do we go from here?" asked Marquen. "I wouldn't mind a nice stream or pond to wash away this mess."

"I believe there is a town nearby that may offer a place to wash in," offered Iviana. "I suppose we'll head that way."

Necoli nodded. "I'm familiar with the area. I believe I know the swiftest route to Allensdale."

"Then by all means, lead us," said Iviana, grateful there was one in their company who knew the land. As she had lived all her life in the small FairGlenn wood, she supposed it came in handy Necoli had pirated the kingdom in his younger days.

The town of Allensdale was teeming with people when they arrived. Asking around, Necoli discovered there was a festival to celebrate the prince's birthday. Moreover, he learned of a public washroom where they could freshen up before continuing on.

Iviana could not wait to be clean, if only to keep from drawing attention. They had already received many curious looks thanks to their bedraggled appearance and she could not be certain if the witch–

hunt Sir Loric had unleashed had persisted after her long absence. She would rather not find out by being clad in irons.

Arriving at the washrooms, the facility was split into two sections: men and women. Once within, Iviana was perhaps a little overly gleeful to discover this was no bowl and cloth washroom, but was filled with a dozen curtained tubs. However, she soon discovered the water was terribly grimy, so she turned to the washcloth in any case.

Satisfied, Iviana informed Nimua she would be waiting outside. On the way, however, her eyes caught on to something that made her stomach drop. Hanging on the exit of the facility was a hand drawn likeness of herself, warning she, Iviana of FairGlenn, was a wanted sorceress. An award was offered to anyone who presented her to Sir Loric, or even the king himself.

What a fine birthday present she would make for the king's son. Was she to be thought a criminal in every world she encountered?

Iviana quickly pulled her hair from its braid and let it fall over her face, proceeding to escape the building where she met the young men outside.

"We have a problem," she informed them.

Darist nodded. "We saw. Where's Nim?"

"She'll be out shortly, I hope."

"If you mean shortly as in now, you are correct," Nimua said as she joined them. "I saw. Lets get out of here."

Iviana swiftly turned to lead them from the town, but in doing so she fell into someone, knocking them soundly to the ground.

"Oh, I'm so sorry," she said quickly, bending to help them back to their feet.

The young man initially appeared annoyed, but upon catching sight of her, smiled easily. "That's all right, sunshine. How 'bout you buy me a drink to make up for it?"

Iviana forced her eyes not to roll. "I have other plans."

"Surely those plans include the tavern. Won't you join me?"

Iviana shook her head. "Sorry."

"Say, wait a minute. You look familiar. Have we met?"

Iviana shook her head as Darist swiftly pulled her away with the others.

"We're lucky this town is so crowded," he muttered as they fled.

"It's slow-going getting through this crowd, though," replied Necoli as he paved a path through the people.

At last they were released from the crowd and into a nearby forest.

"Well, that was a close one," said Nimua a little dryly. "I had no idea that nasty Sir Loric would follow through on his threats after all this time."

"He's a prideful man and she spurned him," said Darist.

Iviana nodded. "This is a very personal vendetta. I wish I had realized the sort of man he was from the start. Might have saved myself from this. We're not much better off than in the Greater Archipelagos."

Nimua shook her head and placed an arm around her. "There was no way you could have known. We were all pushing you. I'm just happy you didn't follow my advice and marry the villain."

"Well, I, for one, would like to know just where we plan to stay this evening," said Necoli. "Judging by the season, I don't recommend we sleep outside."

Iviana nodded. "My cottage is some hours from here, but I think we can make it by sunset."

"Won't your FairGlenn villagers turn you in?" asked Marquen.

Iviana thought this over. She had left the villagers as a well-loved citizen, but it was no secret many believed she used dark arts to heal. Now this witch-hunt had come in to play, she had no way of knowing just where she stood with them.

"Well, we've nowhere else to go and I personally haven't any money to put us up in an inn, even if there wasn't a chance I'd be recognized. Besides, I live in the woods, so it isn't likely they'll notice us there for a night."

Necoli nodded. "It's our best option for tonight, anyway."

Nimua smiled warmly. "I was so disappointed when we weren't able to see the home you grew up in when last we were here. For so long, I've wanted to see that house."

Iviana felt she understood her desire. "It was your grandmother's home."

Nimua's grin broadened. "I never met her, you know. You will have to show me her things."

"Of course. I'll show you her favorite places in the woods, too. Perhaps on our way out tomorrow morning."

⠃⠦

Soon, the travelers passed a sight Iviana had not seen for some time. In truth, she scarcely recognized it but for a large flag in the center of the town. The last time she had seen it, it had been filled with merchants, wares for sale, streaming ribbons and cheerful people. That must have been a special day, she realized, for now the town looked as any other: people going about their business, a handful of those with goods to sell while others hung laundry, dumped waste and wrangled impish children. The spectacle was rather ordinary, but it contained a memory she would cherish forever. This was the town in which she had met Bell, the unusual woman who owned a bookshop with a collection of birds in the yard.

Iviana knew she ought not to enter the town nor should she be so close. They had only done so driven by hunger. Curiously enough, the food they had meant to bring with them from the Greater Archipelagos had gone bad upon passing through the portal. The plan now was to send Darist and Necoli in to procure some food with what little Kierelian currency Necoli yet possessed, then they were to find themselves a peaceful place to rest somewhere in the woods just outside the town.

Those plans were about to be altered.

Darist took quick hold of Iviana's arm as she started into the street. "Just where do you think you're going, friend?"

Iviana turned to him excitedly. "This is where Bell lives—the woman who gave me the book."

"The book?"

"*The* book. The one about the Great One and His son."

Understanding lit his eyes, but he swiftly worked to conceal it. "I can understand your wanting to see an old friend, but you know you can't be here."

Iviana smirked. "It's adorable you think you can convince me to stay behind," she said easily, moving toward the town. She did, however, pull her hair close to her face. Once Darist and Necoli joined her, they attempted to block any direct visual of her.

When at last they came to the plot the bookshop ought to have been, there was, in its stead, a patch of perfectly green grass dotted with flowering weeds. Iviana turned all about, to make certain she was in the right place, but recognized the buildings on either side of the lawn.

"Er... is this your bookshop, Ivi girl?" asked Necoli.

"I swear it was."

"You read fairly interesting books, don't you?" he teased, pulling up one of the nearby weeds.

"The building must have been torn down," Darist conjectured, noting the dismay upon Iviana's face.

She nodded. "Ask someone, will you?"

Darist understood and made his way to the nearest person—a man carting around a barrel of vegetables.

Returning, he appeared all the more confused. "He claims there never was a bookshop in Allensdale, nor a building in this spot."

"None at all? Are you sure? Perhaps he hasn't lived here long enough."

"Says he's lived here all his life, about a block away."

Iviana returned her attention to the small field. She had the book; it was not possible she had imagined the ordeal. Shaking her head, she made her way onto the plot, eventually approaching the place she remembered the small den of birds had been kept and wished she might witness their colorful array once again, not to mention their owner. There were questions she had been dreaming of asking since she had left the woman that day. She had always taken for granted she would be there when Iviana returned. Now, it was as if she had never been.

Darist and Necoli strode up alongside her.

"We asked a few others... They say the same," Darist informed.

"If she's never been here, I shouldn't have that *book.*"

"Perhaps... perhaps it was only *you* who saw her," Necoli offered.

Iviana turned to him. "Well, it certainly looks that way."

"Yes, but... suppose when you saw the bookshop, it was like a portal to another world... a portal only for you."

"In the shape of a shop?" she asked doubtfully.

"Why not? Would you have entered if it hadn't? I mean, it turned out to be pretty important that the Great One got that book to you and we all know He works in ways we may never comprehend."

Darist nodded. "It doesn't explain it entirely, but..."

"But it's the best explanation I'm going to get," Iviana relented. "Well, if that is the case, I was lucky to be fortunate enough to meet her at all. I wonder who she was. Do you know, she was the first person, aside from my mentor, who treated me like I was a *person*, who treated me with *kindness.*"

"It's not as if she's dead," Necoli reminded.

Iviana nodded. Taking in the sight of the vacant

lot one last time, she said, "I suppose we should finish our errand."

The three moved toward one of the vendors on the edge of the town who had been selling fruits and vegetables and procured as much food as they could fit into their bundles. But it was when the older man placed the last of the squash into Iviana's hands that the wind blew casually over the group and swept Iviana's hair from her face in such a way she looked regrettably similar to her wanted posters.

In that moment, the kindly farmer—who had recently come upon hard times—took in the sight of her and with none but his children in mind, made the unfortunate decision to trade her in for the reward. Iviana watched this play out on his face as if in slow motion, and was only partially caught off guard when the man pulled a knife from his satchel.

But Necoli had been watching just as closely and had his dagger pulled in the same moment. Unfortunately, the interaction caught the attention of two knights passing through and it was only Darist's quick thinking and anointed strength that sent them flying in time to gain a running start, though it was not long before the duo was on their tails.

Seeing they were willing to go so far, Iviana

ventured the vegetable man had informed them who she was in an effort to gain the reward. But she knew the man's effort would be in vain, for the knights were out for their own gain.

In their escape, Iviana began to ask herself why she did not simply face them when the three nearly toppled over a large root. Though they were spared, Iviana thought it would be rather fortuitous if the knights happened to trip over that root and inwardly cheered when she heard them do that very thing.

When incidentally they came upon Nimua and Marquen beside a quiet, shimmering lake, they turned to find the knights gaining on them. Iviana realized they had inadvertently led their pursuers to the two who were least capable of defending themselves. They all had their Great Gifts, of course, but they could not blatantly use them in Kierelia, for fear it would place them in further trouble should they actually be caught.

"Uuuh, I say we swim for it," Necoli shouted as he took hold of Nimua's wrist and pulled her under the water.

Iviana wondered why he felt it necessary to make such a desperate escape when she realized the knights had been joined by a bowman who was sending arrows after them. Without another thought, the remaining three dived beneath the frigid water. As they swam toward the other end of the lake, Iviana made out Marquen's form as he reached for Darist to aid him with his Swimmer's gift and Iviana knew Necoli and Nimua were safe, for Necoli was also gifted with breathing underwater, but she wondered how long she would be able to remain below. That was when Iviana halted her swim, for she realized the reason she had not needed to break the surface.

Iviana searched for signs of the Swimmers with her, wondering if they were aiding her without her realizing, but found she was alone. Truth be told, she was surprised neither had thought of her well-being. Nevertheless, *she was breathing underwater.* This was certainly a new development. She had never been able to breathe beneath water before.

Knowing the others were far ahead by now, she could not help but linger, basking in the knowledge she could stay below as long as she wished... whenever she wanted. How was it possible?

She was aware she should be hurrying to the shore, for their pursuers weren't going to wait while she took in this new discovery. Even so, she could not bring herself to move until she realized she might also have the Swimmer's speed. Making certain she was facing the correct direction, she shot forward, cutting through the lake as swiftly as the Swimmers did. It was *exhilarating*, comparable only to flying with Tragor.

All of a sudden, she collided with another speedy being. Finding herself well and whole, she was immediately concerned for whoever she'd crashed into. But the man before her—who appeared at first worried and then surprised as he realized what she had only just discovered—revealed himself to be Necoli. He wasted no time in gesturing for her to follow as he led her to the shore.

Iviana was beaming when they reached it, even as Nimua squealed her fears that they'd lost her. Iviana attempted to explain, but once they were clear of the water, the group fled the lakeside. So caught up in the discovery of her new gift, Iviana could scarcely recall from what they fled.

This wasn't the first time a gift had appeared without warning. She had grown up a Healer, not even aware of the supernatural abilities it entailed. But she had later discovered she was a Seeker as well as a Seer. Iviana caught herself grinning over how infuriated the council would be if they found out about this.

The group continued on until Necoli was

certain they had lost their pursuers. Even so, he repeatedly re-covered their steps, creating false trails and covering signs of their direction. When at last he allowed them to rest, Nimua embraced Iviana.

"Oooh, I was so frightened when you didn't appear at the lakeside with the others. I could have slain these Swimmers for helping me and Darist while forgetting you."

Necoli's eyes widened. "Hey, you're handful enough, lady love."

Marquen only smirked at Iviana until Nimua was forced to ask what secret he kept.

"I think Iviana should answer that."

Iviana blinked. "How do you know?"

"I rather expected it to turn up. Not to mention I sensed something... different... in the lake."

"But you went in after me anyway. I saw you coming up when we did."

Uncharacteristically, he shrugged. "I could have been wrong. Couldn't live with that on my conscience, friend."

"What are the two of you talking about?" Nimua asked at last.

Iviana grinned. "I, um... it turns out I can breathe underwater now."

Nimua's mouth dropped open. "Are you

kidding me? You're a Swimmer, too?"

Iviana nodded, knowing Nimua felt as she did about the gift.

"So, you're *all* Swimmers now?" Nimua cried. "It's not fair..."

"Hello?" Darist waved to her.

"Oh, you don't count," Nimua answered flippantly.

Darist looked to Iviana with a questioning smirk.

Iviana patted him on the back. "Guess you don't count anymore."

"He doesn't count because he can pull a tree up by the roots," Nimua clarified.

"Well, you're a Seer, remember?" Iviana replied laughingly. "That not enough for you?"

Nimua shrugged. "It's better than nothing, but I don't really see much."

"You saw those men chasing us," Marquen put in.

"Seriously?" asked Necoli. "Why didn't you say anything?"

"Uh, I only saw it a few moments before you came tearing through the forest," she defended.

"Well, that was handy," Darist teased.

"So you see my point."

"But hold on, Marquen," Iviana interrupted. "How did you know my being a Swimmer would 'turn up?'"

He smiled knowingly and said, "You're Iviana."

❧ 11 ❧

Iviana

THE TRAVELERS WERE desperately exhausted by the time they entered the FairGlenn wood. And rightly so, as they had spent the entirety of their day escaping one foe or another, constantly peering over their shoulders in fear of some enemy.

Additionally, in their escape from the knights and the bowman, they had spent far too long traveling in the wrong direction, forcing them to make a wide circle back in hopes of missing their pursuers. With nerves overstrung, not one of them had found the capacity to eat. Needless to say, they were bone-weary and hungry, which did not make for the most pleasant traveling companions even among the best of friends.

At last, deep into the evening, Iviana raced ahead of the others as the small one-room cottage of her childhood came into view, set aglow by moonlight. Making her way up the walk that was now overgrown with weeds and garden, what was left of the climbing roses waved their sweet scent in welcome. Swinging the door open, she swiftly lit the nearest candle and lifted the sconce to look about the large room.

Everything was as she had left it except for one old toy on the floor beside the fireplace. Iviana stooped to pick it up, wondering where it could have come from, then checked for dust about the room. Finding none, this was her answer. The toy belonged to the child of her dear friend Merri, who had kept the cottage clean in Iviana's absence. This was a sure sign Merri had not turned on her.

How Iviana wished she might visit her, but she could not alert anyone to her presence; she could not even leave a note, for fear others would learn she was in the area. Even so, Merri would likely guess if she noticed things moved.

Presently, the others entered, looking rather ragged. Iviana quickly set about making them comfortable and preparing a quick, filling meal. It was unfortunate there were only two small beds in the place, for the young men would have to sleep out in the shed. Thankfully, it would be filled with piles of dry hay.

Iviana chanced the fireplace to fix a meal of cooked oats, dried fruit and fresh cream from the cow that had been well milked in her absence. There was a possibility someone would see the smoke billowing from the cottage, but at this late hour, it was unlikely. Besides, they needed a warm meal after their day of fleeing the troubles of their worlds. Cool glasses of freshly dipped well water were added to the quaint meal, satisfying every one of her companions.

"Ivi, this place is so cozy," Nimua commented contentedly as she stretched her lanky body across one of the beds.

Darist nodded vehemently. "It's too bad we can't stay a while."

Necoli and Marquen nodded their agreement.

Iviana grinned, thoroughly warmed by their compliments. She had often longed to show her home to Nimua, Darist and Flynn, knowing they would love it as she did. But, of course, Flynn was missing. And what a mess everything had become. Being in the cottage and away from the Greater Archipelagos suddenly made her long for his companionship. But as there was nothing she could do about it, she determined to rid her heart of him.

"Are you all right, Iviana?" asked Marquen.

Iviana made herself smile. "Only tired."

"Then we'll leave you ladies to sleep," said Necoli. "I noticed you have a decently roomy shed. Don't suppose you've tried it for sleeping?"

Iviana shook her head. "But I imagine it'll be fairly comfortable. Let me get you some bed things."

"Don't trouble yourself," said Darist. "We brought them along, remember?"

Iviana nodded. "I'm still not letting you sleep in there without all the necessities of household living."

She proceeded to fill a pitcher of water that they would have ready drink at any hour. She then found an armful of extra quilts and pillows she and Naphtali had made through the years. Finally, she left some candles and the leftover dried fruit in case they grew hungry in the night. At last, Darist pushed her into the house and closed the door firmly that she would enjoy some much-needed rest.

"I've been going through some of these night things," said Nimua, rummaging through a trunk. "I don't suppose you'll mind my borrowing something. Nothing I brought is really warm enough for this climate."

"Of course not. I can find you something of

your grandmother's, if you like." Pulling a long pink one from a chest of drawers, she held it out for Nimua to see. "You should keep this. I know she would love you to have it. It was her favorite. She said it made her feel like a lady in a castle."

Nimua's eyes began to water, but she quickly blinked the tears away and dressed herself.

"Thank you," she said with meaning.

Tears were nearly drawn to Iviana's eyes as she realized it had been some time since she had really thought about Naphtali; she still missed her deeply.

Laying claim to the bed she had chosen earlier, Nimua said, "Now, shall we chat about things girls do when they sleep over with one another? Being so far away from my mother makes me feel like gossiping."

"That's because your mother doesn't abide it."

Nimua nodded. "Lets see... have you any beaus here you haven't spoken of? Of course, if there is anyone you haven't told me about, I'll be terribly irritated, but do spill."

"Oh, no, there's no one. It's a small village and I certainly haven't been looking. Besides, I was an outcast here most of my life, remember?"

"But you said that changed."

"Yes, but there's still no beau."

Nimua frowned. "You're dull," she said with a yawn. "Oh, never mind. I think I'll sleep. Be sure and wake me in plenty of time to spruce for Necoli."

Iviana made a disbelieving noise. "As if you need sprucing. You awaken looking just as angelic as when you fell asleep."

There was no reply but the deep, steady breathing of her slumbering friend. Iviana chuckled and tucked herself into the bed that had been her mentor's. Falling into much needed sleep, she breathed in the scent her mother-like friend yet present in the sheets, though they had been washed many times.

Soon, Iviana was astonished to find herself standing across the garden from Naphtali, who was in her gardening apron and gloves. The woman turned and gave her a look as if Iviana had been daydreaming again instead of doing her work.

Iviana shrugged, smiling, and began pulling weeds.

"You've neglected this garden," said Naphtali.

Iviana looked about and wondered why she had done so. She could not understand why her heart was pained with this. "You are right," she replied sorrowfully. "I'm sorry."

"Don't be. It means you have begun to truly live

and I so want you to live a full, love-filled life. It was not fair I allowed you to grow without companions your own age and I am sorry for that. We should have started over elsewhere."

Iviana shook her head fervently. "I needed no friends. You were more than enough."

Naphtali stopped her gardening and appeared thoughtful. "I believe you. Still, I'm glad you've made friends. I see you no longer need me and I'm glad."

Iviana ran to Naphtali and took hold of her wrists. "Of course, I need you! I've needed you since the day you left me."

Naphtali gazed deeply into Iviana's eyes with her own stormy gray ones. She brushed the stray hairs from Iviana's face and caught the tear that escaped her eye. "I was so lucky to be given you for a daughter. I can't wait until you join me here in Paradise. We will have marvelous times, we two, but you have much to do and it will be some time before we are reunited. I love you, my sweet girl."

Iviana was shaken awake.

"Ivi, you must wake up," cried Nimua.

Iviana reluctantly peeled her eyes open. "Oh, what is it? I'm dead tired."

"But it's nearly noon and there's someone

here."

Iviana anxiously sat up. "Noon?! Who?"

Nimua gestured to the young woman who stood smiling at the foot of her bed.

"We all slept in, it seems," said Nimua regretfully. "I don't think the others are even awake yet."

Iviana smiled widely at her friend Merri and quickly stood to embrace her. "What are you doing here?" she asked.

"I might ask you the same," Merri replied. "I came to use some of the old hay from your shed and found a group of men there. I thought about shewing them out, but decided it had been an understandably cold evening and I would make them a little breakfast instead... but here *you* are. I'm so glad you're back. We've a good deal to talk about. Honestly, I can't believe you'd even chance coming here, but I'm glad you did. The village has decided to stand beside you in this silly witch-hunt. We want to protect you, if we can."

"Oh..." Iviana gasped in her surprise. She had not expected such loyalty from the town. *"Everyone?"* she asked a little skeptically.

"Every last man, woman and child of speaking age. We love you Miss Ivi and won't have anyone taking our healer away. Of course, when you were gone so very long, we often wondered if they had already nabbed you, but when the search continued, we were comforted you were yet free."

Iviana was overwhelmed by this news. The Great One certainly worked in mysterious ways. "Truly, I don't know what to say," she admitted.

"Say you and your friends will remain here, if you like, and we will guard you and be certain your presence is not discovered."

Iviana hesitated. "I don't know. I will have to discuss it with my companions."

Merri grinned. "Of course. Now, I think my little ones have just gone to awaken the strangers in the shed now they have learned they are your friends, so I'll start on a meal for you all. Sleeping in so late, you must be famished. Where have you come from, anyway?"

"Oh… we ran into a little trouble elsewhere."

"My goodness, what an adventurous life you must lead. And staying at the house of the famous Sir Retrom and his Lady Laurel, attending banquets and balls and the like—from what we've heard in rumors. I'd have never thought it of you when we were growing up, at least not since you returned after Naphtali's death."

Merri prattled on while she began the meal, but that name gripped Iviana's heart agonizingly. If only she had not been awoken, she might have had more time with Naphtali, even if only in dream. It had felt so real.

"You look pale, Ivi," said Darist as he and the other young men entered with armfuls of children. "You should sit down."

Iviana did not obey. Rather, she stole a few garments for Nimua and herself and drug her out to change in the shed.

"Your friend is very agreeable," Nimua commented. "And how wonderful are your FairGlenn people? What a change from what you said you grew up with... and from what we've just fled."

"Yes," Iviana replied absently.

"Are you all right? Darist was right; you do look pale."

Iviana shook her head. "I'm fine. It's just hard being back here."

"It's making you think of Naphtali, isn't it? It is me, too. I wish I'd have known her. My mother has told me so many stories about her. She must have been exceptional."

Iviana nodded, but said no more.

Upon returning to the house, they were met with the scene of Darist, Necoli and Marquen playing a game with Merri's four adoring children. The twins, a couple of lovely red-haired girls, ran to Iviana and embraced her legs, exclaiming how much they'd missed her. They then turned to the stunning Nimua and embraced her as well. The slightly shorter of the two asked to sit on Nimua's lap. Upon consenting, her lap was full of children.

Iviana aided Merri with the meal of thick, hardy carrot and potato stew, a tray of freshly baked honey rolls and a large bowl of various dried fruit and nuts with honey to spoon over. Iviana was relieved there was no meat to be had, as Merri would not have known her friends did not consume it. As it was, the group of other-worlders loved the stew with its fresh Kierelian herbs. It pleased Iviana to see them enjoy the humble offering.

After they'd finished their meal, Darist quietly pulled Iviana aside. "Your friend seems very nice," he said, "but what are we going to do now? Shouldn't we get out of here while we can?"

"I was meaning to speak with you all about that," said Iviana, turning so the room could hear. "Merri has told me the villagers have taken my side in this ordeal and they will tell no one I am here. If you all agree, I was thinking we might remain here—at least until we can find other arrangements."

Darist's face brightened. "Well, that is wonderful news! I, for one, would love to stay a while."

Nimua had, of course, already been informed of the news, so it was the affirmation of Necoli and Marquen that set the plan.

"How wonderful that we can stay in *your* house," said Nimua when it was agreed. "I was afraid we would be camping around like the last time."

"I do wish I had better place for you all to sleep," she added for the sake of the young men.

"Are you joking?" asked Necoli. "We slept so soundly we didn't awaken until these kiddies started poking us."

Marquen agreed. "I felt a strong presence of the Great One over this place—a blanket of serenity. I believe that is why we slept so agreeably. I feel as if I need never sleep again."

ᚼᛒ

After Merri and her children left them, the comrades discussed their plans and dispersed. Iviana wished to show Nimua some of her grandmother's favorite flowers and trees, Marquen and Darist took the initiative of pulling the numerous weeds from the garden and Necoli desired nothing more than to enjoy a peaceful nap out on the soft, grassy hillock where Iviana's cow grazed.

So, a peaceful day was planned for all until, upon Iviana and Nimua's return, they discovered a line of people outside the cottage door. At the sight of the young women, Darist raced over to inform that most of the village was there either to bring her welcome gifts or for healing of ailments and illness.

When Iviana approached her line of neighbors, they quickly encircled her, calling out exclamations about her long absence, wondering what sorts of adventures she'd been on and how she was fairing. This was all wonderfully healing to Iviana after having been chased from the Greater Archipelagos. She merrily proceeded in examining her patients while she expounded upon all that had happened with Sir Loric and the witch-hint. She was astounded to see many of the young women sigh, wishing it had been them in her stead. Unable to understand what he had truly been like, they romanticized Iviana's stories, stowing it away for dreaming.

By the time Iviana had bid the last of her visitors

farewell, it was long past a decent supper hour and her stomach growled demandingly. Fortunately, Darist had taken the initiative of preparing a meal. She had only to enter the cottage with Marquen—who had helped with the patients—to be greeted with large plates, filled with enough food to feed far more than were living at the small cottage. Even so, Iviana rapidly cleared hers.

"I can't believe those same people rejected you and Naphtali your whole life," commented Nimua as they finished.

Darist nodded. "I know. Hard to believe from what we saw today."

Iviana chuckled contentedly. "The Great One really changed things when I returned from your world. Even their memory of Naphtali is more than favorable."

"Then the Great One will keep us safe here until... well, until..." Nimua's words trailed off.

The others looked on in confusion, but Iviana understood. Until when? Where were they to go from there? She had led her friends from their own world into hers and in doing so may have ruined their chances of returning home. She wondered if the council had already locked the door against them—if *Flynn* had set the portal to deny them.

But what *was* to become of those within the mountain? In her cowardice, she had abandoned the people's plight and with her absent, who was going to save them... if anyone? She held little hope Flynn would rouse from his idiocy and handle the situation as he should.

Iviana's stomach churned with the emotions these thoughts triggered—feelings of betrayal, hopelessness and confusion. It was as if a drape had been pulled across her vision and she could no longer see a way forward.

↢12↣

ERA

ERA LINGERED UPON a bench on the edge of the Atlantian dome and watched the colorful array of sea creatures glide over the protective field. It was a beautiful sight—her favorite, in fact—but it did nothing to soothe her.

Not only was she disturbed she had failed in getting anyone to take her dream seriously—which clearly explained the Chosen One's absence from the realm—but it was maddening knowing about the prisoners and not being able to do anything for them. Even if she could get someone to believe her, she didn't know the prison's location, thanks to the fact she'd never been above.

The question that plagued her most was why she had been shown the mountain-prison in the first place. Why *her*, of all people—a girl whom no one would believe because she was only fourteen? Granted, she hadn't attempted to tell many people. The Island Leaders were the only ones who could really do anything about it, but her parents would not allow her to see them. Without their support, the leaders probably wouldn't give her the time of day.

After a few days, Era had lost interest in talking about it. She was weary of being treated like a child. Worse yet, she was beginning to believe they were right—that it really had been only a dream—and that notion made her ill.

It wasn't as if she desired people to be unjustly incarcerated. She just wanted the dream to *mean* something. It had affected her too deeply. If the scenes had not been reality, then might not the dream have some meaning for her, some message from the Great One? But it seemed the dream-interpreter could not even give her that.

The problem was, even as Era attempted to move on, it held great weight in her heart. Again and again, she attempted to lay her burden before the Great One, but it would not lift. As a result, she experienced nightmares that she had been incarcerated herself. And Iviana the Chosen One never came for her.

"Era?" Aedis interrupted her thoughts. "Are you all right?"

Era put on her best smile, realizing she had allowed a few frustrated tears to drain from her eyes. "It's nothing. I'm fine. Just been emotional lately."

Aedis eased herself onto the bench. "It's the dream, isn't it?"

Era could not help noting a difference in Aedis' tone, as if she was ready to listen. "It is."

Aedis sighed. "I'm sorry I haven't been more willing to take you seriously, Era. I've been busy with this new project the Kais have asked me to focus on. I haven't really been there for you."

"It's not that exactly. It's just... Oh, I can't explain it."

Aedis peered into her eyes. "Would you try? I want to help, if I can."

"It's... a number of things. It's no one believing me to the point I'm beginning to doubt it myself. But even if I forsake it, I feel the burden weighing on me like a curse. And then the Chosen One being absent..."

Aedis nodded. "That, I understand, but... surely she'll return when the time is right."

Era nodded, but it troubled her more than she liked to admit. "What if..." Dare she ask it? "Aedis, what if she *doesn't?*"

With those words, Era's world began to spin until she could no longer make out her surroundings. Flailing her arms about, she attempted to reach for Aedis or anything that might ground her. She began to feel as if she would pass out when, quite suddenly, the spinning ceased and she fell upon the ground.

Pressing a hand against her racing heart, she muttered, "Oh, Aedis, I don't know what happened. I became terribly dizzy."

When there was no reply, she opened her eyes and looked to where Aedis had been only moments before, but she was gone. Gazing about, Era discovered not only no sign of Aedis, but no sign of Atlantyss. She was somewhere else entirely.

She was... *above.*

Above the surface of the ocean with dark gray clouds fuming overhead, she could not believe how dissimilar it all was to all the sunny scenes she had seen in her classes and on the walls of some of her friends' homes.

Not only was the sky gray and murky, but the ocean was adorned similarly. This, she knew, was not right, for she had seen more of that ocean than any Swimmer could brag; she had lived within its depths and knew well what a brilliant golden-blue it was, how it glistened even far beneath the surface. The body before her should be that same brilliant blue. She had even heard tell the water was crystal clear upon the shore. Instead, it was murky. Not to mention, what should have been white sandy beach was a pasty mire that now clung to her leggings.

Where could she be if not the surface of the Greater Archipelagos? It was apparent she was on an island. There were several others surrounding, making it clear she was in the center of a series of archipelagos. But what had happened to the world she had barely known—the world she had not before been given the opportunity to know?

And how had she gotten there?

As amazed as she was that she had somehow involuntarily transported, she could not help feeling disappointed by her initial view of the world above. She would have preferred to remain in her grand, underwater city than to experience this dark, murky and utterly uninviting world.

Still, she *was* above.

After attempting to clear some of the sludge from her clothes, she noticed some buildings inland and headed in their direction in hopes of finding a means to clean herself—not to mention, perhaps discovering some answers. Moving shakily, she found herself anxious to meet them, for her Atlantian instructors had warned her of their ways. After all, Era had always assumed she would experience it after the Great One's plans were fulfilled and the people changed for the better.

Even so, it was not long before she was forced to confront her fears, for it appeared as if an older couple were headed in her direction. When the woman took notice of Era, she appeared to be studying her with great interest. Without warning, the woman broke into a run, headed straight for her. Naturally, Era's first thought was to flee. But there was something familiar about the one flying toward her.

As the woman, who looked to be in her sixties, drew near, she slowed, taking careful steps toward Era, searching her face as if to discover some answer.

"Era?" she uttered at last, unbelieving.

Era studied her more closely. The woman *was* strangely familiar, yet she did not recognize her. At last, she nodded, admitting, "I am Era."

The woman released a long breath and studied her further, attempting to confirm her discovery.

"I don't suppose you had a mother named Era?" she asked.

Era shook her head. "My mother is Raphshi."

The older woman shook her head in disbelief and at last the man who had been with her joined them.

"She says she is Era, but..."

"Can't be," said the man. "She doesn't look a day over fourteen."

Era couldn't help giggling at his certainty since she was, after all, herself. "Well... I *am* Era."

Suddenly, Era caught a familiar wrinkling of the forehead on the face of the man that immediately reminded her of Merrick. Turning to the woman again, she realized who she was facing.

"Aedis?"

Aedis' eyes grew wide. "Era, how can it be you?" Her eyes began to well with tears. "I thought we'd never see you again! What happened to you?"

Era had no answers, no words... for if this was truly Aedis and Merrick, she had somehow—*no*.

"I have no idea..." she replied breathlessly, goosebumps racing up her arms. "How long have I been—er—gone?"

"Since the day you were telling me of your troubles, your dreams that were not dreams after all, but living nightmares."

Era's stomach sank. "Then I was right... but oh, I do not understand any of this."

Era's body began to shake with the reality of her situation.

"Oh, you poor thing. We've frightened you and I see there is more to this than can be readily explained. And look at your clothes. Well, come home with us. We'll get you cleaned up and try to get this whole thing sorted. I really cannot tell you how overjoyed I am to see you again. You have no idea how losing you has plagued me all these years. I could never cease wondering what had become of you."

"Oh, stop talking her ears off, Aedis. She's as white as a sheet," said Merrick in a tone that sounded nothing like the one she had known when he was a boy her own age. It sounded, if she had to describe it, devoid of hope. But Merrick had always been a dreamer.

Aedis, too, was changed, but her generous heart was still vastly apparent as she took warm hold of Era's hand to lead her along the path.

Era could not help wondering what her friends were doing on this island and why their appearance was so... bedraggled, their clothes patched over and over. Their expressions, as well, had lost all vibrancy. These were not the Aedis and Merrick she had expected when they reached their maturity. They should be spectacular leaders in world culture, great Inventors, admired and respected by all. Instead, they appeared almost homeless. This theory was disproved, however, when they led her up to the door of a small building that looked as if it might have been beautiful at one time, but was currently quite filthy and in disrepair.

"I know it isn't much..." Aedis admitted as if reading Era's thoughts.

She opened the door to welcome her into what looked to be a two-room residence, which was, in its small way, somewhat cozy, if dingy, decorated with old furniture that was as patched as their clothing.

Aedis proceeded to lead Era into a bedroom where she offered her another set of gray patched clothes and left her there to change. Alone, Era's mind swirled with questions. Firstly, how was she *there*, in what seemed to be *the time to come,* if Aedis and Merrick's age revealed anything. Apparently, she'd missed years—since the day that had been mere minutes ago for her. As she threw on the provided clothing, the thought of her parents filled her mind and she fled the room to ask.

"Oh, they... passed away, I believe," Aedis admitted. "Though I confess I have not kept the best of tabs on them since they were sent so far from here.

After all, it is difficult to keep in contact with other islands since the dragons were sent away. But I am so sorry, dear."

Era refused her apology. Her parents were not dead in her time and she refused to accept their death now. "Sent away?" she questioned, taking the seat provided for her.

Aedis and Merrick looked her over with some concern. "Oh, where have you been all these years?" Aedis asked.

"Nowhere. I only just arrived here when you found me. Moments before that, I was speaking with you... *younger* you."

Merrick's mind appeared to race with this information. "You moved through time," he said at last.

"Is that really possible?" asked Aedis.

Merrick nodded. "It is. I remember tales of another who moved through time, though he was considered an old myth when we were kids. It was considered a Great Gift, I believe, but by our time the story had been presumed fictitious. Pity," he said, looking Era over with new interest. "What a gift to research—"

"Don't," Aedis said gently, placing a hand on his knee to quiet him.

They looked into one another's eyes for a moment before Merrick glanced to Aedis' hand and placed his own over hers. That was when Era discerned their relationship.

"Are you two... *married*, or something?"

"We are," affirmed Aedis with a small smile.

Era had not seen that coming. "But you're so much older than Merrick!" she cried, clapping her hands over her mouth as the words were uttered.

Aedis giggled softly. "Only by three years. I suppose that seemed a great gap when we were young, but things... change as you grow older."

Merrick flashed Aedis a quick smile and squeezed her hand lovingly, then returned his attention to Era with concern. "Era... I'm afraid you're not safe here. If you plan on remaining in this time, we must find a way to get you away from this realm, onto Kaern."

Era's stomach turned. "What do you mean?" She didn't want to remain in *this time*. She had to get back to her parents, her life and her friends before they were old and in love.

"If truly the last you knew was of that day so many years ago," Aedis began, "you have missed a great deal."

Era nodded. "Tell me everything, beginning

with why you think I'm in danger."

Aedis stole a long breath. "Because of your gifting... if indeed you are a traveler of time."

"But what is so improper in that?"

Aedis raised a brow. "Come now, even when we were young the council would never have permitted someone with that gifting to live freely. Because of your dream, you understood before any of us what the council was doing to those whose gifts were deemed 'hazardous' to the community at large."

"Yes. They were imprisoned. They're actually doing that?"

Aedis nodded. "That and much more. Although, I suppose there's less imprisoning now. That prison was only so large and this was a world full of gifted people."

"Was?"

"What would you say if I told you an Inventor and a Healer were commissioned by the council to create an elixir that would neutralize a person's Great Gift?"

Era gulped. "I would say I hope beyond hope that is not true."

Merrick responded with a bitter smirk.

"How?" Era cried. "When?"

"We heard rumors of it not long after your disappearance," Aedis explained, "though no one really believed it. Eventually, however, the nightmare made itself reality. Not long after, the lost Isle of Atlantyss was discovered."

"Yes," Merrick added, "discovered and the inhabitants forced from their homes to be questioned, punished, imprisoned, brainwashed and have our gifts stripped from us by what is called Kurnin's Elixir."

"But why? Why would someone create such a thing? Why was Atlantyss treated so?"

"Oh, it wasn't only Atlantyss. It was just about every island on the face of our planet. The Realm Leader and his council raised up the Enforcers, people who were willing to commit whatever crimes the council asked of them."

"But how did they get people to consume this elixir?"

Merrick stared off as he continued, "Various ways. Some took it without a fight, knowing there was no way out. But then there were, as I mentioned, the Enforcers: those who are gifted to force people into slumber, at which time they inject the elixir into their system. Others have gifted strength and you'd be surprised how much that intimidates people, at least after a few beatings."

"Where in the world did they find people like that?"

"As far as we know, the council had been raising them up in secret for some time, training them, brain-washing some from their youth. There are even a group of people called cannibals who were a large help during that time.

"After years of numbing the anointing of those whose gifts were considered unfit—even some of the gifts that had formerly been embraced—we find ourselves here, giftless, living from the pitiful rations supplied by our ever generous council."

Era could not believe her ears. How had all this been permitted to endure? Why had her people not risen up? Yet... she understood. The council and their Enforcers had oppressed the people until they were what she saw before her: hopeless, dreamless and dead inside. Whatever had happened over the years had been devastating. It had broken them— even these two who had had so much promise in their youth.

"What of Flynn, the Realm Leader? What did they do with him?" she asked.

"Nothing," Aedis replied. "He is the current Realm Leader. Though, I'm not certain he is quite deserving of that title anymore. They say the agelessness a Realm Leader is anointed with has begun to fade from him, that he is beginning to age, and rather more rapidly than I suppose is pleasant."

"Oh, who cares?" Merrick broke in bitterly. "He's been the council's pawn since day one, so they say. Maybe with him gone, we can finally get the people to rally around raising up a leader of our own, one who will stand against the council and free us from their unendurable rule once and for all."

There were a few moments of silence before Aedis asked, "But *who?*"

Merrick lowered his head, rubbing the back of his neck as if it ached. "*Who?* You are right there, dear one. Who in all this world has the strength of will and heart? Who has not been overcome by the oppression that hangs over us? Even the sea and skies..." He looked up to Era with such intensity it nearly hurled her backward. "Did you know that even the sea has begun to swallow us up, that some of the islands have begun to flood until their people have had to be evacuated?" He dropped his gaze, rubbing at his neck again. "It's as if we're—"

"Cursed," Aedis supplied. "We all know it." She looked to Era. "I believe it is because of what you saw that night, Era. Those people were imprisoned and we allowed our council the freedom to perform such an act; our people trusted in them far too much. I wonder… if we had done something back then, might everything be different now."

Era felt as if she might cry. If only she had been able to convince them. *Could* they have done something? But she had not been the only one who was aware. There was yet another who had been far more involved than she.

"What about the Glory-bringer?" she asked quietly, almost fearfully.

Merrick did not lift his gaze, but Aedis replied, "She hasn't returned."

Era's head pounded. Had something happened to Iviana or had she truly chosen to remain safe and secure in that other world?

"I remember you saying something about it that day you disappeared," Aedis went on. "You were right. You knew better than anyone."

"But that can't be," Era contended. "The Great One *chose* her. It was prophesied for over a hundred years she would come and—"

"But she didn't," Merrick said angrily. "Either we heard wrong or…"

"The Great One has not forgotten us," Aedis assured him. "I know it. I feel him when I do the washing, prepare food, as I go about my day. He fills me with such peace, if only for small moments. He still cares. *We* made our choice and we have brought a curse upon ourselves we never dreamed."

Merrick breathed heavily. "We can't let them do it to her, Aedis. How can we get her out?"

"Why not the door?" Era asked. "Why has no one escaped through the door into Jaela's Cavern?"

"They reprogrammed it," Aedis explained." It doesn't let anyone in or out without Flynn's input into the system."

"Next you'll be asking about the dragons and their portal in the sky," said Merrick. "But they were forced to leave years ago. Only a handful escaped with them. Sure, they were powerful and all, but they had only stayed by the approval of our people. So, when they were commanded to leave, they humbly submitted as only the most powerful of creatures will. Obviously, they did not want a fight—knew they'd win. For whatever reason, they did love us."

"Then you're truly trapped," Era said hopelessly.

Merrick smirked. "So are you, young one, and with such a gift as yours, I pity you." He froze suddenly before, "Then again... can you not use it to escape from here?"

That thought had not occurred to Era. She had no idea if she even had such a gift or if she had arrived in this future by some other means. Still, if there was a chance she *could* traverse time, she knew precisely where she would go.

"How would *you* suggest I go about doing that?" she asked them, knowing even if they were oppressed, they were still two of the greatest minds on the planet.

"Hm..." Merrick began. "Transporters were able to move from place to place by the mere thought of where they wanted to be. Might you not try it that way?"

Era supposed it was worth a try. With a glance at the two old friends before her, she said, "Great One, please take me back."

With that, her world began to spin. When at last it slowed once again, a pair of arms were thrown about her. "Era, what happened to you?!" Aedis cried. "You disappeared and I was so frightened. I was just about to fetch your parents." Suddenly she pulled away and asked, "What are you *wearing*? You weren't in these rags before." At last, she peered into Era's face and saw something of the depth of what Era had learned. "Are you all right?"

"How long have I been gone?" asked Era.

"I don't know, a minute? Maybe less. But you disappeared before my very eyes. I've never seen anything like it. What happened?"

Era looked into the youthful face of the older girl. "Oh, *Aedis.* I've got to see the Island Leaders."

ಣ13ೞ

IVIANA

FOR AN HOUR each day, Marquen attempted to teach Iviana how to call forth water as he and the Swimmers had when they'd faced the dark dragon. For whatever reason, that hour always ended fruitlessly and it was beginning to wear on Iviana's nerves.

"*Why* can't I get this?" cried Iviana. "Brenna and Necoli had it in a matter of moments!"

"Well, they were faced with a terrible beast. I imagine desperation had something to do with their results."

"Then attack me and we'll see what happens."

Marquen grinned widely. "One, I do not attack people. Two, I find it hard to believe you would view me as enough of a threat."

Iviana looked him over. "Well, you were pretty

intimidating when we faced the dark dragon. Still... you may be right."

Marquen grinned. "Lets give it another go. Repeat the steps aloud."

Iviana stole a deep breath and released it slowly, taking a determined stance. Holding out her hands, she said, "Connect with the Great One." She looked toward the sky with a smile and said, "Hi." She continued with, "Call the water from His presence..." She drew herself from her stance and turned to Marquen. "Maybe the problem is I can't picture Him. I've never seen Him."

"You've seen His son. Picture him."

"Ah," Iviana said with raised brows. "That could work." She repeated the steps and pictured the Anointed One. She imagined the water flowing into her person until it rushed through her arms. Finally, she thought, *release...*

"Nothing..." she said to Marquen.

"Hm." He rubbed his brown-bearded chin. She was again struck by the fact that, beneath those whiskers and despite what his character displayed, he was not much older than she was. Yet, he seemed ages wiser. It really wasn't fair.

Without warning, a large blast of water shot over her with such force she thought her skin would bruise. As it ceased, she looked to Marquen, from whom it had come, and sent him a severe scowl.

Spitting out the liquid that had sprayed into her mouth, she took her stance and, without another thought, succeeded in blasting Marquen, drenching him from head to foot as well as the trees and foliage surrounding him. She then stood back, blinking as she realized she had accomplished her goal.

Instead of responding in turn, Marquen only smiled. "I wondered if that would work."

"Well, it was *my* idea. I thought you doubted it!"

Marquen laughed heartily. "But, you see, it was the element of surprise that brought results."

Iviana turned from him and raced back to the cottage to meet Darist and Nimua where they worked in the garden. In her absence, it had overgrown and sprouted many unwelcome weeds. Since most of the plants were foreign to all but Necoli, Iviana had taken the opportunity to teach them about Kierelian plant-life and it had intrigued them.

"You did it?" Nimua asked with bright eyes.

Iviana embraced her and nodded. "Marquen fooled me and it worked."

Nimua giggled, but Darist was surprised.

"Really?" he asked a little laughingly. "I wouldn't have expected it of him."

"Neither would I," Iviana replied laughingly, "But I don't care so long as it was successful."

"As Marquen would say," began Nimua, "'Whatever achieves results.'"

Marquen nodded as he approached. "If I'm not careful, you'll know all my secrets, Nimua, and then I'll be useless."

Nimua made a doubtful noise. "Except you're the keenest Seer since Latos. If only you'd been made Realm Leader—" Nimua cut her words short and looked sorrily to Iviana.

Not wanting to raise questions, Iviana changed the subject, "Oh, I see someone is coming. I believe it is that young man for his mother's medicine—the one we prepared this morning. I'll see to him myself."

Over the past few days, Iviana had been training Marquen and Darist in the ways of healing. Though they did not have the Healer's eye or touch, it had never occurred to anyone that some of the things Healer's knew could be learned by anyone. As Marquen and Darist showed so much interest—Marquen in the actual process and Darist in simply being a help—Iviana had taught them several things they could manage themselves. Once they were finished, she would bless the person with her healing touch.

During this time, it interested her how differently the FairGlenn villagers responded to the purple glow that came with her Healer's gift. Iviana recalled how Naphtali had often asked her patients to close their eyes while she touched them, so as not to raise suspicion or fear. But there had been times when someone had caught her at the wrong moment or when parents had been there to see their child healed. This had been the chief reason the villagers had feared them. Of course, they had always been intimidated by their medicinal procedures, but the purple light was simply too peculiar for comfort... back then.

Now, word had spread of that purple touch and the peace and warmth that came with it. Many looked forward to it, eager to see it for themselves. In those moments, Iviana began to take the time to explain from Whom it was supplied. Though many accepted her tale about the Great One and the sacrifice of His son, they saw it as just that, beautiful tales. Even so, there were others who took it to heart and it delighted her she could introduce more friends to the Ones she loved so much.

Meanwhile, as Marquen and Darist bandaged wounded arms and legs and prepared treatments, they also began to tell stories and it wasn't long before many came simply to hear them. Sometimes, they would even speak about a world apart from Kaern, the Greater Archipelagos, where people with special powers dwelt. These stories, Darist told himself, shocking Iviana with his candor. Especially when some began to look at her questioningly, wondering if she, with her Healer's gift, could be from that miraculous world of islands and ocean. They began to see her as a hero of a grand fairytale—the creature of a beautiful, foreign world.

Much as she hated to admit it, the stories Darist told were slowly mending her heart toward that world that currently held only painful memories. He reminded her of the things that were *great* about the Greater Archipelagos, the things that were worth saving, if possible. But then she would recall the way Flynn had refused to aid her. She attempted to think of a plan that would save those people without getting any of them killed by cannibals or other means—means she did not wish to explore—and her feelings toward that world would sour again.

Then, of course, there was the distraction of everyone in town thinking her and Marquen were a couple, for they were often seen walking and talking together, never-mind how often Iviana attempted to put them straight. Marquen was not at all affected by it, saying they could believe what they chose, but he did not plan to marry. Even Iviana wasn't certain she would ever do so, but the rumors still bothered her.

Late into the evening on the day Iviana mastered calling forth the water, she sat idly with Nimua in the window seat and confronted her with this.

"Can you imagine me and Marquen? I mean, I have a great deal of love in my heart for that man, but I can't say my feelings would ever go *that* far."

"For some time, I've thought you and Darist would make a match," Nimua admitted as she gazed out the window.

Shocked by this, Iviana looked up at her friend. "*Darist* and I? Of course not. That's almost worse. They're my *brothers*."

"Well, it was just a hunch. You should be proud of me for not having played matchmaker."

"Oh, I'm more than grateful. How embarrassing would that have been?"

Nimua chuckled. "Well, if you decide to remain single for the rest of your life, utterly devoted to *our* friendship, I'd be perfectly happy."

Iviana chuckled. "Nimua, I may remain single,

but I cannot promise I will not completely move into your married home. In the least, you may find me there six days out of seven and your husband will certainly despise me for eating you out of house and home, not to mention stealing all of his angelic wife's time."

Nimua grinned. "Sounds lovely to me. Now, what do you say we put talk of men behind us and sleep. Tending your garden has been more tiring than I expected."

Iviana agreed and lay in her bed, thinking of the events of the day and attempting to sort out just what was in her heart only to find it all hopeless. Finally, she fell into a deep sleep. And within that sleep, she began to dream.

She dreamed she stood over a young girl in a bed unlike she had ever seen and the room was comprised of walls and tubes that reminded her of a place she had thought of often in the last months. Iviana stood still, attempting to ascertain whether or not she was dreaming of the lost Isle of Atlantyss, when the girl in the bed suddenly turned, widened her eyes and squealed at the sight of her.

Sitting up, she demanded, "Who are you? What do you want with me?"

Iviana was contemplating the latter query

herself, but she simply responded with, "Er–I'm Iviana."

Era blinked. "Oh, you're—you're the Chosen One, aren't you?"

Iviana paused a moment before nodding.

"How did you get here?" the girl asked, standing excitedly to her feet. "You came back! Oh, I just knew you would."

"Well, I…" Iviana rubbed her arms, attempting to determine if she was only dreaming or had transported in her sleep. She had, after all, had other gifts appear from nowhere, making her a Healer–Seeker–Seer–Swimmer, but it seemed she was not a Transporter, for she felt nothing beneath her fingertips. "I think I'm only dreaming."

The girl weighed this, reaching out for Iviana's arm, but her hands went right through them. "I see…" She tried this on herself and achieved the same result. "It appears I'm dreaming, too, then."

It was Iviana's turn to study her. "But this feels real, doesn't it? I have had something like this happen before… I connected with another in my dreams."

The girl nodded. "Now you say it, so have I. I went with you, but you did not see me."

Iviana was taken aback. This was all a bit

uncanny. "What is your name?"

"Era."

Iviana nodded. "Well, where did we go in your dream?"

Era's face grew solemn. "I saw the prison in the mountain."

"You did?" Iviana asked numbly.

"I've also seen the future. You have to come back."

Iviana looked her over. Who was this girl? "What happens in the future?"

"It's terrible. The council takes over everything and I mean *everything*. The Great Gifts are extinguished, our freedom and independence are ripped away, Atlantyss is discovered and evacuated and Aedis and Merrick get married."

"Aedis and Merrick?" Iviana asked, surprised. "That's terrible?"

"Well... no, not that part."

Iviana nearly smiled, but the remainder of what Era had revealed was working its way into her consciousness. "How do they do this? Why don't the people *do* something—in the very least, escape the realm?"

"I'm not altogether certain. The council breaks their spirit with something called Kurnin's Elixir, designed by an Inventor and a Healer to remove the giftings. Then there are the Enforcers, a team I believe Kurnin and the council have been assembling. It's made up of men and women who are willing to enforce the elixir on the unwilling. Then they're going to banish the dragons and lock the door to Jaela's Cavern, so there's not much chance of escape once that has been done. I don't know any more than that. I was there a very short time and spoke only with Aedis and Merrick when they get old... Oh, you just *have* to return and keep it all from happening."

Iviana grew ill, her ears pounding with indignation for what was to come. Her mind raced as she considered all she'd heard— particularly Era's last comment. "But... but if you've *seen* the future; isn't that *it*. That's what the council does. It ruins everything. That *is* the future of the Greater Archipelagos." Suddenly, a thought that made her heart beat wildly struck her. "What about Flynn?"

"He's..." Era began.

Iviana could tell Era understood the effect her answer would have on her, for she was almost frightened to reply, her eyes lining with tears. It grew difficult for Iviana to breathe until at last Era admitted, "He's still the Realm Leader. But it's not as if he was the mastermind; they called him a pawn. Still, he locked the door."

"A *pawn?*" cried Iviana bitterly. "*As if that's any better?*"

Somehow, it was worse. It wasn't *Flynn*—not the one she knew. But then... that Flynn did not appear to exist anymore. That thought, now utterly confirmed, made Iviana's heart and stomach twist together until she thought she would break. That was when the vision of Era's forlorn face began to flicker, as if Iviana was blinking. Then, the wooden planks of her cottage ceiling were above her.

Era was within her reach no longer.

For hours, Iviana sat thinking. Her mind reeled with thoughts of Flynn, the prisoners, the mysterious Era and her tale of the future. Her stomach turned over and over. She knew with more sleep she would be able to see it all more clearly, but try as she might, she could not quiet her spinning thoughts in order to enter into slumber.

Many times, Iviana looked over to Nimua in her bed, wishing she would awaken so Iviana could share it all with her. At last, when the sun began to peak over the horizon and send tiny glowing fingers through the cottage windows, Iviana stood over Nimua's bed and whispered for her to awaken.

Nimua peeled her eyes open discontentedly. "What is it? Is something wrong?"

Iviana sat on the edge of her bed. *"Yes."*

Nimua sat up quickly and rubbed her eyes. "What is it?"

"Everything: Flynn, the council, the future of the Greater Archipelagos. It's all so messed up."

"I know, I know," Nimua said softly.

"No, you don't. There's *more,* if my dream was... more than a dream."

"Tell me about it."

"I met this precious girl named Era from... well, from a place I never told you about. I'm not supposed to; it's a secret place in the Greater Archipelagos. Somehow, she followed me to the prison on the cannibal island. And she's seen the future. It seems everything that could go wrong does. The council and Kurnin go power-crazy and... Flynn goes with them. Everything beautiful about the Greater Archipelagos is going to be ruined."

"Hush, now," Nimua soothed. "I'm sure it was only a dream. The Great One would never let that happen."

"But what if He has no choice? What if it was *our* choice—the Greater Archipelagos? What if it was cursed and... what if it was my fault?"

"How *could* it be, Ivi?"

"Era claimed I must return to somehow fix things, but... if that *is* the future, I don't see how I can change it."

"Ivi, I—I don't know what to think or tell you..." Nimua said, at a loss. "What are you going to do?"

That final expression on Era's face would not leave Iviana's thoughts for a moment, plaguing her like a stubborn housefly. Era meant something to her, but she could not say just why. In any case, she could not disregard her dream, real or no. "I don't know yet. I must speak with the Great One."

ɞ14ଔ

ERA

ERA AWOKE THE moment Iviana disappeared with the disparaging feeling she had made a mess of things. What if that had been her only chance of getting the Chosen One to return? She kicked herself for not having handled it better, but could not think of another way.

Iviana would not return, for she believed the future could not be changed. That thought filled Era with the deepest fear she had ever known. But what if Iviana were to come back, after all? Wouldn't that alone change the course of the future? Still, she had not agreed to return—had practically refused.

The future was unchanged.

Seeing the dome's light growing brighter, Era swiftly dressed. She had an important meeting to attend—possibly the most significant of her life.

Thanks to Aedis' having seen her disappear, it had not taken long for Era's parents to take her seriously when she revealed everything to them the evening before. With them behind her, she would not have to face the Atlantian Island Leaders on her own, for they insisted on setting it up themselves and accompanying her. They tried all they could to arrange a meeting with the Island Leaders that evening, but it had inevitably been postponed until the following morning.

Walking through the halls of the underwater city's main edifice, Era grew dreadfully anxious. Would they believe her story? Or would they think her an adolescent girl in desperate need of attention? Worse yet, would they think her unhinged?

Finally, they were before the room in which they were to meet and her father knocked upon the door. Era entered shakily when they were welcomed inside and it was all she could manage not to flee when those in the room looked at her with confusion, as if she was not meant to be there.

"Oh, er, we understood we were to meet with the two of you alone," said one of the leaders to her parents.

"No, this meeting is our daughter's," her father explained.

Not wanting to unsettle anyone, Era offered shyly, "I suppose my parents could just tell you."

"But I'm guessing it has nothing to do with them, does it?" asked the man she was later told was Ferrol. He stood and met them at the door, welcoming the small group into the room and offering Era a congenial wink. She was immediately put at ease.

Next, she was introduced to the women who were standing beside their seats. The younger, whom Ferrol introduced as Jephran, wore an intimidating expression that made clear her time would not be misused. Mae, the elder, looked more lovely than anything, with fluffy white hair and a sweet smile especially for her.

"Come and sit beside me, won't you?" the elder woman asked.

Era immediately did as she was told, grateful to be saved from having to sit near the more intimidating woman. Her parents and Aedis took their seats as well.

Jephran made no secret she was bothered by Aedis' presence, but said nothing aloud.

"Now then," began Ferrol in a pleasant tone. "Will you not begin, Era?"

Era was at first unnerved by the eyes of the room

upon her, but closed her own to determine where to begin. "I dreamed I was with Iviana the Chosen One," she began.

Ferrol and Mae's faces displayed immediate interest. Jephran's remained blank, waiting.

"But I do not believe it was a dream, exactly. It was, perhaps, a vision or... Well, I followed her to an island I have never seen before... obviously."

Even Jephran revealed a small dimple at this. It was well-known the youth of their city knew nothing of the world above.

"Within one of the mountains was a prison. I believe that prison exists."

Ferrol sat forward in his seat. "A prison for...?"

"People whose powers are considered dangerous by the council."

"You believe the council created a prison for their own people, a people who have not committed any crimes?" Ferrol clarified.

"That is what I understood," she replied a little shakily. "It was Iviana speaking with them—not me."

"What did she do?"

"She ran out. I believed at the time she meant to do something about it, though the people there warned it was dangerous."

Ferrol looked to Mae a moment and then to Jephran. The two shared a moment's unreadable thought.

At last, he turned to the rest of them. "I believe your instincts are accurate, Era. I wonder if this had something to do with why the Chosen One fled our world. I only wish we knew more."

"Well..." Era hesitated.

Mae laid a soft, warm hand over hers. "I see you are a young woman of mature character. We will listen to all you have to share."

This encouraged Era, but only a little. What she had to say might make them change their minds about believing her. "Well... er, there is a little more."

"A little?" her father muttered

Era continued before she lost her nerve. "Something odd happened to me yesterday, but Aedis can vouch for me, I think."

Aedis nodded and said, "To begin with, she disappeared before my eyes."

Ferrol sat up in his seat again.

"I... I think I somehow traveled into the future, *our* future—that is, the future of the Greater Archipelagos. There, Iviana did not return. Or, at least, had not yet done what she was prophesied to do. She did not save the people in that prison... and I think she's the only one who knows where it is who would be willing to help."

Upon further prodding, she revealed the whole of her story, causing Aedis to blush once more over the news she and Merrick had been married. But by the end, Era had even the unwavering attention of Jephran.

"And they said Iviana had not returned, but could not say why..." said Jephran. Turning to the others, she added, "Any chance she is in some danger? Is there something we can do?"

Era had planned on telling them of her dream encounter with Iviana just before waking that morning, but thought better of it. She wanted the people in this room, the only ones who had the power to do something, to have hope. They simply could not give up as Iviana had. If they knew what the Chosen One's opinion had been, they may do just that. Era could not bear it. No matter how set the future seemed to be, they must *try*.

"There has to be," said Ferrol. "That is a future I cannot bear to see through."

Jephran turned to Era with the full force of her powerful person. "I wonder if you could point out the island on a map."

"I don't think so," she admitted. "But I'll try anything." Of course she would try anything. She was just astounded these notable people were so willing to take her seriously.

Jephran and Ferrol immediately stood to fetch a pile of maps and spread them over the table. The entire room proceeded to gather around them, pulling any details Era had to offer and combing through every map. Unfortunately, when it came down to it, the number of islands was too vast.

Jephran sat down in a huff and turned to Era. "Well, you can move through time, young woman. Could you not transport yourself there?"

"I'm not sending my daughter into a dangerous prison, if indeed she is even capable of doing so" insisted Era's father.

"He's right," said Ferrol. "That's too risky. There has to be another way."

"Did I hear something about time-travel?" asked a woman leaning comfortably against the doorframe with her arms crossed.

"Chamaeleo," gasped Ferrol. "Thank the Great One you're here." Turning to the room, he continued, "If anyone can sort this out, it's her."

Entering the room, the woman said with some amusement, "Don't count on it just yet. I have to know what we're dealing with before I determine to be impressive." She winked at Era, reminding her of Ferrol. "Now, who, may I ask, is our Time-jumper?"

The room turned to Era.

"Um, that's me," she admitted.

Chamaeleo's eyes lit up as she made her way over to Era, taking the seat beside her and turning it to face her. Leaning in close, she murmured, *"Fascinating."*

Era blinked back at her as a smile broke over her face.

"The girl has seen our future..." said Jephran. "And it looks disastrous."

Chamaeleo grinned. "Oh, that wasn't our future."

"What do you mean?" asked Era self-consciously. Had she been wrong about everything?

"If that was our future, she would not have been taken to see it," Chamaeleo explained. "Obviously, we're going to change it."

Era noticed Mae grin as if she had understood this all along. *Why didn't she just say so?* wondered Era.

"But she's discovered some terribly underhanded dealings of the council," continued

Jephran.

Chamaeleo halted her with a wave of her hand and gazed into Era's face. "I don't want to hear about that—not yet. Right now, I want to hear about Era."

Era liked this woman.

"So, you're a Time-jumper," stated Chamaeleo. "Do you know there has only been one other known Time-jumper in all our history and he has begun to be considered legend? You have just debunked that theory, I am extremely satisfied to say. I have always been partial to the idea."

Era's insides lit up with her words. She had not considered appreciating the gift until that moment. "Then it is a Great Gift?"

"Certainly," Chamaeleo said easily. She sat back in her chair, folded her arms behind her head and propped her feet upon the table. "My question is... *why you?* And I don't mean to say you are not worthy—only that I think there may be some reason. If you have been shown something specific that will affect the future of this world, why did the Great One choose to entrust it to Era of Atlantyss?"

"Well... I don't know," Era replied honestly. Surely, others would have been better suited for the task.

Chamaeleo swiftly drew her arms and legs back into their proper positions and said, "No matter. But know this: There *is* a reason. *You are* special, Era... one of the Chosen Ones."

Era's eyes nearly welled over. She had so looked up to Iviana, dreamed about the prophecies surrounding her... now this superb woman had given her the same title. This woman thought *she* was special. But why?

"Now... there are, of course, other things I wish to discuss about your gift, but it seems I'll not have heard all unless I allow you to tell me your story."

With that, Era began to share her journey into the future for the third time. Checking the clock, she made herself thankful that at least she was not sitting in lectures. And when she had told all—including every detail, for this woman did love details—Chamaeleo the Shifter took charge.

"All right, gang," she began. "Firstly, we locate Iviana. We're not doing this without her."

"But she is in another world," Era reminded. "How will we find her?" She did not mention finding Iviana was nearly the last thing she wanted done if these people were to remain hopeful.

The room was silent until Ferrol recalled, "Oh, of course... this Time-jumping Era is also a Seeker."

Chamaeleo smiled. "A Seeker who can time-jump? That should be interesting." She stood then and headed for the door, turning in time to say, "Hop up, Seeker. You're coming with me."

Era stood, briefly meeting the anxious glances of her parents. "Where are we going?" she asked as she followed Chamaeleo through the door.

"Kierelia of Kaern. Hope you're comfortable with heights."

ᘓ

"Pick one," Chamaeleo said as they faced three large, almost bored looking dragons.

Era gulped. "Why don't we take nelepyres?"

"You know very well nelepyres aren't allowed out of the city. Now, go and introduce yourself."

Era stepped up to the mighty creatures—the ones she had always been intimidated of—and said, "Uh, hello... I'm Era?"

At the sound of Era's voice, one of the dragons looked up and met her gaze. She was struck by his bright green eyes and could not seem to pull herself from them.

"Really?" Chamaeleo asked as she saw the two looking at one another. "That's certainly surprising.

Well, hop on, Era, dear."

"Why are you surprised?" Era asked as she forced herself to draw nearer to the bright-eyed one.

"He doesn't like people. I was only bringing him along for Iviana."

"What good would he do Iviana if he doesn't like people?" Era asked, newly intimidated by the fact this dragon should not like her but seemed to anyway.

"Well, he likes *her*, but apparently you're an exception as well, so *get on*. I promise he won't bite... as far as I understand."

Era forced herself closer and placed a hand on his muzzle. As he did not seem to mind, she proceeded to stroke it gently. When he made no threatening movements, she moved to his back and finally pulled herself up.

"You know who he is, don't you?" Chamaeleo asked as she sat grandly upon her own dragon.

Era shook her head.

"That's Tragor, the Great Dragon of the Ages."

Era paused where she sat, holding her hands out awkwardly, uncertain of what to do and a little afraid to move. "The Great Dragon of the Ages?" she squeaked as she peered down at his neck. "Are you sure I should ride with him?"

"If he likes you, you'll be fine."

"What if we misread the signs?"

Her words were wholly ignored for, with the wave of Tragor's mighty wings, they began to rise. And, though Tragor moved gracefully, it was a great jolt to Era. Immediately, she wrapped her arms around his neck and held on for dear life.

As they continued rising, Era realized her eyes were closed and she forced them open to gaze wonderingly at the world around her. They were in the midst of some of the tallest buildings in Atlantyss. And in no time at all, they were above them.

Just in time, Era spotted her parents, Aedis and Merrick waving to her from down below and she loosed one hand long enough to wave wildly in return, suddenly regretting not having given them a proper farewell. It was not as if she was leaving for good, yet it felt permanent somehow. With that realization, she kicked herself for following Chamaeleo at all, for leaving the city—and without her parents' permission, no less. In all the times she had dreamed of leaping upon a dragon and escaping her bubble, she had pictured herself much older, not to mention inevitably fearless.

As the colorful buildings of her fair city gleamed far below and the dome was just above their heads,

Chamaeleo warned her to take a deep breath. At that moment, Era truly wished she could fly off the back of the Great Dragon of the Ages and be caught up in the arms of her mother and father.

Clinging to her mighty dragon for all she was worth, she shut her eyes against what was to occur: the bending and stretching of the dome as they pressed through and then the wild rush of gushing water all around them. All at once, Era was back in her childhood nightmares, her city flooding and drowning. Sensing her terror, Tragor moved with great speed and had her free of the ocean before she knew it.

Quite suddenly, the world was not so heavy anymore and they were flying free and clear over the ocean that concealed her home. When Tragor had righted them and was flying smoothly just below the clouds, Era took a few moments to catch her breath before she absorbed the planet below that was, at first, only blue. Even so, she was so grateful to find it was not the terrible murky brown that it would be in future if they did not alter the timeline. Oh, but the water was so different from this view, moving a little less languidly and rising over the beach on the nearest island in frenzied chorus.

Suddenly, Era felt an indescribable warmth flood

her body and she tore off her jacket, searching for the source of the light illuminating this world only to find it blinding and glorious. At last, she released her grip on Tragor's neck and fell backward onto his spine that she could stare up at the fluffy white clouds illuminated by the fiery sun. Once she'd had her fill of the sky, she sat up and gazed down at the island below, studying what she could of its intricate green plant-life and white beaches, of its mountains...

"Now, then," began Chamaeleo. "How do you like your first experience outside Atlantyss?"

Era giggled, surprising herself. "It's everything I hoped it would be." She took a deep breath and then sniffed the air. "It smells so different. Almost sweet."

"Honey," Chamaeleo supplied. "The water is filled with it and its scent seeps into everything on the planet."

"Oh, how peculiar. I like it."

"Now, if you don't mind—and I do realize this is your first flight—but I would rather like to make haste. Might we speed along to the sky portal in an effort to get to Iviana as soon as possible?"

Era grew tense at the mention of speed, but the quality of the air was different outside her domed city and filled her chest with courage. "Very well."

With that, Tragor shot forward so speedily, she

nearly lost her breath. In fact, she found it difficult to breathe until she learned to bury her face in Tragor's neck where the cutting wind could not reach her.

They flew in this manner for some time until they were suddenly roaring through a swirling vortex. Era was surprised to find herself filled with profound wonderment, though she knew she would ordinarily be terrified. Instead, the swirling portal held the atmosphere of delirious, unsubdued potential and it flooded her with thrilling exhilaration until they were released into a cloudy blue sky, not unlike the one they had just left behind.

"Oh, my," Era whispered as she laid eyes on the parched earth below, devoid of plant-life and begging for sustenance.

"It's a wasteland," Chamaeleo explained. "It would be rather useless if it was not for the fact that it provides privacy for this portal, making it safe for dragons to use. Unfortunately, they're considered a formidable enemy because of the dark dragons of old."

"I see. Does that mean we are in Iviana's kingdom? Are we in Kierelia?"

"Well, my dear, it is not exactly *Iviana's* kingdom. It is, I suppose the king's, er, this land's leader."

"Like Flynn?"

"Sort of... but not quite so grand. The king only rules over a small portion of the planet. The rest is either governed by others or unclaimed."

"So, the planet is divided?"

"Yes, I suppose you would say that."

"That sounds terrible."

"It's not exactly terrible," Chamaeleo said with some amusement. "Though it does make things rather more difficult, doesn't it? Well, I suppose they make it work the best they can. After all, they cannot fly upon dragons in this world, so it is much more difficult to travel."

"Because they do not trust the dragons. How silly of them. If they would only give them another chance, they could see so much more than they planned. They might even grow more united."

"Perhaps, or it might just cause more problems. Anyway, there are yet dark dragons among them, so they are far from trusting any dragon at this point. Therefore, we must fly a little higher to keep ours safe from harm."

"What could these people do to a mighty dragon?" Era asked, finding the thought humorous.

"Believe it or not, they have the weapons for it. I know such things are scarce in the Greater

Archipelagos, but here, they are used on a daily basis."

"That sounds dreadful. Why would Iviana want to live here?"

"*My*, you ask a *great* many questions, but that is one, I'm afraid, you will have to ask her. And after all, our world has its problems too, as you well know. Now, as you are the Seeker here, I am counting on you to lead us in the right direction. How are we doing?"

It donned on Era this was the first time she had been given the chance to search for something of substance... not to mention outside of Atlantyss. Closing her eyes, she stole a moment to feel for the sparking energy of the Seeker within her blood and found their course already correct.

Through their flight, Era worked hard to remain silent, though her mind was flooded with questions about this new world. She kept herself busy with the realization she had not only experienced her own world for the first time, but had entered yet another within the same day. This was something she was certain few could claim, if any. She would certainly have a story to take back with her.

Realizing she had done at fourteen what not even Aedis had been allowed to do, she hoped she would get the chance to escort Aedis and Merrick to Kaern one day.

Then, at last, Era was struck with a question she simply could not deny. "Why do you think I was chosen, Chamaeleo? Why have I been included in all this and why do you think I was able to have that dream meeting with Iviana?"

"Dream meeting?" Chamaeleo raised her brows in surprise. "Are you a Dream-walker?"

Era blushed, realizing she had divulged her secret. "I could be wrong. It may have only been a dream. I wish it had been, to be honest. There is reason I did not share it." She felt almost as if she might cry over the memory.

"I believe it was genuine, that you truly met her in your dream," Chamaeleo ventured. "Else you would not feel so emotional about it."

Era contemplated whether she should fill Chamaeleo in on the details of it in order to warn her of what they might discover when they found the Glory-bringer.

"I have my... suspicions," said Chamaeleo.

"About what?"

"About why you would meet Iviana in a dream, why you are being used in all this."

"And they are...?"

Chamaeleo looked her over carefully and actually hesitated, something Era had not yet seen her do. "I do not know if it is my place to say."

Era blinked back at her. "Not your place? Why not?"

"That is… Well, it's fairly complicated."

Era shook her head. "I don't care how complicated it is; I must know."

Chamaeleo appeared as if she was weighing this. At last, she released a sigh and said bluntly, "I believe Iviana is your birth mother."

Era stared back at her, winded, wide-eyed and speechless. At long last, she was able to mutter, "How do you even know I was adopted?"

"I recall a meeting I was in when you were younger, about you being a Seeker, I mean. I learned then you were found within the city without any trace of your parentage. Your adoptive parents found you and fell in love, thus given the rights to keep you."

Era nodded, appearing calm, but filled with turmoil and confusion, a great number of questions and doubts racing through her mind. "But… isn't Iviana not old enough to be—"

"It's not that simple."

Era raised her brows. "Well?"

"In a city like Atlantyss, where you're all trapped there under the ocean, secrets just aren't possible. I'm sure you know that. There's no way you belonged to anyone there without someone being aware. So... how did you get there?"

Era stared back at her while she thought. At last, she followed her gut. If she was correct, her life had been far more eventful than she'd believed. It just couldn't be... "You think I time-jumped there. Oh, goodness, you think Iviana hasn't had me yet—that she's going to have me someday and I'm going to inadvertently travel back in time and well, here I am..."

Chamaeleo nodded slowly. "*Accidentally, not accidentally*... who knows?"

"Well, if I was a baby," Era defended, "I couldn't have done it on purpose."

"No, not you."

"Iviana?"

"Of course not. If you knew the details of her life, you would never think that. No, the Great One. He knew what we'd be faced with at this time and I think, for whatever reason, he decided he needed you here now more than anywhere else. Like I said, *you*, Era, are special... and not just because you're Iviana's daughter."

For hours, Era silently contemplated all this, a wide variety of emotions swelling in her heart. When at last they had drawn near to where they would find Iviana, to the place she was now horrendously panicked to face, she said, "You're not going to tell *her*, are you?"

Chamaeleo did not conceal her astonishment. "Not if you don't want me to, dear."

Era nodded. "I don't... not yet. You don't even know if it's true." At this point, Era almost hoped it wasn't.

Chamaeleo tilted her head back and forth. "Well... I sort of do, sweet one." When Era revealed her confusion, Chamaeleo admitted, "The Great One."

ಬ15ಣ

IVIANA

ALL THE WHILE Iviana and Darist prepared breakfast, Nimua watched Iviana closely. The others stole glances as well, but assumed she had not slept well. They had no idea of the burden she carried, of the choices that needed to be made this day. They yet knew nothing of the reason they had fled their world. Iviana wondered once again why she did not tell them. Their safety was no longer threatened. Leaving with Iviana and Nimua had made it appear as if they knew all. The answer came down to the fact she simply did not want to speak of it.

She had been biding her time.

Their meal complete, Iviana informed them she needed to be alone for a while and the others assured her she need not leave, for they had things they wished to do elsewhere. All but Nimua and

Marquen cast her wondering glances, but they said nothing. Iviana had no idea what Marquen did or did not know. As always, he had the tact not to breach the subject.

After Nimua and Necoli left for their venture, Marquen and Darist made ready to leave as well. After Marquen stepped through the threshold, Darist turned back once more, as if he might ask what troubled her after all, but seemed to change his mind with a small smile before closing the door behind him.

Iviana released a long sigh as she turned away from the door, releasing the pent-up emotion she had been attempting to conceal not only that morning, but since they had fled into Kaern. She kicked herself for not having faced the Great One before—not like this anyway—and wondered if she had feared what He would say. Facing that thought, she could not guess what was on His mind, but she owed Him the question and He owed her the answer, so she felt.

At last, she asked, "*Great One*, what am I to do?"

And then she waited. But much like the evening of the Time of Waiting when she had heard His voice for the first time, He did not at first answer and so she voiced her question again.

"Oh, Spirit of the Anointed One, what is to be done? Please answer me, for I cannot bear to face this without your voice."

With that, she broke down, shedding the tears she had been reigning in for too many days. She got down on her knees and held her stomach as she wept, awaiting the Great One's response. But even unto her final tear, there was nothing—not a word softly spoken into her spirit, nor any sign of the spirit dove; she received no visions. But she had learned the Great One did not always answer one in the way or the timing expected, so she determined to wait in the cottage until He was ready to speak.

While she was yet on her knees, tear stains hot on her cheeks, someone came flying through her door and knelt down on the floor before her where she proceeded to pull her to her feet. Looking up, it was Merri.

This was not what Iviana had expected.

"Ivi, I ran here as quickly as I could," she said breathlessly, holding Iviana by the shoulders. "We must go. Sir Loric and his men are here to claim you. Someone has betrayed you, betrayed us all."

Iviana spared no time to ask questions, instead heading straight for the door, but as her fingers grazed the handle, the sounds of shouting and horse's hooves sounded outside, likely trampling the garden she and her friends had worked so hard to sort, the garden she and Naphtali had spent so many years planting and nurturing.

"Quick, hide!" Merri cried. "I will tell them you have escaped."

But before Iviana had a moment to decide how she could conceal herself, the door flew open and Sir Loric stood within its threshold.

"Where is she?! Where is Iviana the witch?" he demanded of Merri.

When she did not answer, Iviana watched as, slowly, his eyes found hers. Why had she thought she could remain in one place without putting herself and the people she loved in danger? Even now, her friends might return any moment and be caught. Closing her eyes, she reached for the blade at her side, knowing she was outnumbered, but refusing to go down without a fight.

Sir Loric shouted again, halting her movement.

"*You!* Don't touch that!" He marched over and stole her sword, tossing it carelessly behind him. "Where is the witch?" he spat.

Iviana blinked into his face. Did he not recognize her? Had she changed so much in the time

229

they had been apart? Studying him, she was reminded of the coldness of his piercing blue eyes. Oh, how she hated that she had ever thought of caring for him. Nevertheless, he appeared just as she had left him, though his nose *was* a little crooked from when Flynn had socked him.

"If you are hiding the witch, you will be slain here and now," he muttered coldly.

That was when Merri turned to Iviana in confusion. Her eyes widened at the sight of her. What on Kaern had happened?

"We..." Merri said, new light in her eyes. "We forced her from our village only this morning."

Loric peered straight into Iviana's face, squinting his own to appear as dangerous as he could. "Does this woman tell the truth?"

Iviana nodded. She had no way of knowing what was going on, but followed Merri's lead. "We were making ready to purge the place of all her... witchcrafty... materials. Don't want to have any part in the devil's dealings. She's deceived us long enough."

Loric turned on Merri then. "You should have turned her in to me," he said angrily. "Do you know in which direction she went?"

Merri nodded. "I believe south. Toward the

main road, I would guess."

"Very good," he said.

Without another word, he fled the premises to continue his hunt for the woman who had rejected him.

The two women who remained caught their breaths a moment before Merri finally turned to Iviana questioningly, "Iviana... it *is* you, isn't it?"

Iviana peered at her as she lifted her sword from the floor and replaced it. "Of course, it's me. What is the matter?"

"You... Iviana, I have no idea how you did it unless you truly are some sort of sorceress, but you've changed your looks." Pulling a piece of Iviana's hair before her face, she said, "Look."

Attempting not to cross her eyes, Iviana obeyed, then took hold of the lock herself. "What...? It's red!"

"You look like you could be my sister. Truly, you look like a twelve-year-old girl.

Iviana looked down at her body and found that not even her clothes were her own. "H-how?"

She supposed she should not be entirely surprised. This sort of thing had been happening often of late. But why should she look so much like Merri? "You know, I was thinking of the village, of

231

your children, hoping they were safe. I wonder if it somehow... Well, I don't really know how to make you understand. I can assure you once and for all that I do not use sorcery."

"Well, will you change back? It is terribly disconcerting."

Iviana closed her eyes and pictured her previous form. "Oh, please go back," she pleaded aloud.

At that moment, Marquen entered the cottage, shortly followed by Darist.

"Iviana, we have to get you somewhere safe," Darist cried, running to take hold of her hands which she thankfully recognized as her own. Of course, Darist would not have addressed her so if she had not been herself.

She looked to Marquen and realized he had seen her change, his eyes sparkling with amusement.

"Well, are you coming?" Darist cried.

Iviana turned her attention to him. "They have already been here and gone again. It is all right. I... shifted, somehow, and we told them I had fled to the main road."

Darist dropped her hands and sat on the nearest chair, obviously relieved. Wiping the sweat from his forehead, he asked, "You shifted? Like Chamaeleo? How?"

"I don't know…" Iviana replied.

For whatever reason, it upset her. Days ago, she had discovered she could breathe underwater. Before that, she was a Seer and Seeker and then of course there was her healing. She knew she should be delighted, but it was all—everything within the last week or so—too much.

"Marquen, what is going on with me? Why do I keep gaining all these gifts?"

He stepped toward her. "I believe you're being prepared—filled—with something… for something. You feel different every time I am around you: *fuller.* The new giftings are only a result of it, I think."

"Prepared for what?" Iviana asked with some dismay.

"To return for the prisoners, of course," Chamaeleo said as she entered, followed by Era.

It was almost surreal that the two happened to turn up in that moment. Iviana dropped to the chair beside Darist and took hold of his hand for support.

"Please, come in," she said, almost dizzily. "Take a chair and tell me why you have come. Is it to bring me back? To change the future? You may think I'm some Chosen One, but I am only a girl, *just one girl.*"

She watched Era search her face, as if looking for something that would make her more than a girl. Iviana assumed she had not found it when she dropped into a chair much like Iviana had the moment before. Of course, if the two had traveled from the Greater Archipelagos, they must be tired. Iviana knew she should offer them something, but Darist stepped up for her.

"Nothing for me," Chamaeleo said.

"Could I have some water?" Era asked a little shyly.

Darist offered her his most friendly smile and said, "Care for a little food, too?"

Era could not help smiling in return and nodded. "Thank you."

With that, Darist pulled together what he could for Era, and Marquen excused himself, saying he wished to intercede with the Great One outside.

With that, Chamaeleo turned to Iviana. "What are you doing here?" she asked, a little scolding but genuinely curious. "From what I gathered in the town, you're a wanted fugitive who was nearly arrested just now."

Iviana shrugged. "They think I'm a witch. Well, the town doesn't, I don't think. Not even sure if Sir Loric really believes it, but he wants me to pay for—"

"For denying him," Chamaeleo finished. "Yes, I recall how he watched you. A terribly unsettling man. But you have not answered my question."

Iviana stared into her face. "I feel certain you know why. Still, I know you want me to say it, so I will. I... I guess I am running away."

"Running away? Is that all? I suppose that's understandable, so long as you plan on running back. Precisely what are you running from?"

"I assume Era's told you about the prison? I went to Flynn about it. I even went before the council. They responded by chasing me off the planet."

"Flynn the Realm Leader, I presume. That handsome boy? Why, that must have been heartbreaking."

Iviana did not know how to respond, for, in fact, it had been.

"I wonder if, in truth, you're running from *him*?"

Iviana shook her head. "He is nothing to me anymore."

"But he was your friend—you helped make him Realm Leader. *That* must mean something, at least."

Iviana nodded, relenting. "Of course, it does.

Chamaeleo was quiet and Iviana wondered if she realized their conversation was going nowhere so long as Flynn was in it. Thoughts of Flynn seemed to cloud her mind with rage, but also, admittedly, with heartbreak.

"You know, Ivi, I could have been put into that dungeon."

Iviana looked up at her. "Why?"

"My gift was seen as unfit—too fearsome. As a child, I made the mistake of morphing into the form of Rhimesh. It was meant only to be a joke and, in truth, it caused no trouble except to myself. It was only the fierce protection of my parents that kept me from being sent away. I only know this because my father was on the council and I often eavesdropped on their meetings—that meeting was no exception, of course.

"Though my parents managed to save me from that fate, I was kept nearly under lock and key in my own home. When I was allowed outside, it was never alone and all watched with fear or judgment in their eyes. I was... a bit of a monster to them, I'm afraid. Shifters were extremely rare." She explained this with great emotion, as if she was that little girl again.

"But when I was fourteen, my parents passed

and I was left alone and unprotected. That was when I knew I had to leave, why I lived the rest of my life in Kierelia until the Great One called me back to do what I could in secret. And to work with Atlantyss until the coming of the Great One's plan was displayed in that world.

"His plan is *not* to hold those people captive; you know it as well as I. You know that fearing a gift of the Great One is foolery, blasphemy in itself. There is deep, sinister oppression building over the Greater Archipelagos, circling especially over our capital island. Despite its dazzling bright skies and perfectly white walls, I believe the people have been feeling it grow for some time."

"The Greater Archipelagos is a joke," Iviana scoffed, as if she could contain her resentment no longer

"The Greater Archipelagos was a gift created by the Great One out of the deepest love of His heart," Chamaeleo contested.

"But the Great One knows everything—I know Him well enough to know that now. How could He create a land that was going to become this—this place that rejects and imprisons those He loves and blesses with such brilliant potential?"

"Iviana, have you never heard the story of why

He created that world?"

Iviana grew curious, despite herself. "No."

"Well, the story, as I know it, goes something like this," Chamaeleo began.

Her tale originated long before the kingdom of Kierelia was dreamed of and the people of that land were yet ungoverned. At that time, there lived a woman named Jaela, whose heart was very near the Great One's and His to hers. She was His first friend on the planet Kaern and she vowed every piece of herself to Him and He the same. Still, He desired to give her more. So, He looked upon the stars and knew what He longed to do. One day, He took her and her husband by the hands and led them to a cave, revealing He had carved something exceptional into the end of it.

Jaela looked up into His face with an adoring smile, pondering what the surprise could be. She knew from prior experience it would be nothing short of just who He was and He was *marvelous*. Turning to her husband with that same smile, she raised an intrigued brow and stepped into the cave.

She had no light with which to see, but the Great One provided this with His glory and so they were guided by the sparkling wonder of His presence. Jaela giggled with delight and attempted to touch the shimmering glory with her fingers, but it fluttered and danced around her, into her fingertips and through her hair. She looked upon her Great Friend and shook her head in disbelief.

When the couple reached the end of the cavern's passage, there was a glimmering, shifting veil. The sight of it would have frightened most people, but not these two. Jaela smirked and stepped through the vortex. When she reached the other side, she and her husband found a vast desert land.

"What is this?" she queried, though the Great One was nowhere to be seen.

His voice emanated from the sky with bubbling joy as he said, "It is yours, Jaela. I made it for you. It is all yours."

Jaela's mouth opened in wonder as she took this in. This was a *new world* and, though it was plain, it was *hers*. She fell to her knees and began to weep. "How *great* is Your love for me?" she muttered through her tears.

As a single tear dropped upon the sandy earth, a great, blue substance shot forth from it and covered the land with a vast ocean of the bluest blue water. Jaela and her husband laughed in amazement as they swam in the ocean that now covered the entire planet.

The Great One said joyously, "As wide and deep and great and vast as the ocean surrounding, that is my love for you."

He proceeded to lay a finger upon various areas of the water where beautifully green flourishing islands formed, covered with flowers, trees, mountains and creatures that roared, buzzed, crawled and flew. Some were foreign, while others were familiar to Jaela.

She saw all this and fell beneath the ocean's surface in wonder of it all, but the Great One shed His glory light upon her again and raised her from the ocean, saying, "*This* is my love for you, sweet one. ***This is my love for you.***"

He gently placed the couple upon the soft green grass of the nearest island and stretched out beside them with His head rested upon His bent up arm. "How do you like it?" he asked eagerly.

Jaela released a great laugh through her tear-filled eyes. "I think it will do," she muttered with gleaming delight.

The three laughed together and discoursed until the new sun set upon the land and the uniquely designed stars and galaxies unveiled themselves above.

"In those first moments in that new realm with the love of His heart," Chamaeleo continued, "He *could* see what was coming. He knew the world would eventually be filled and its people as numerous as the stars. He knew every person that would be born into that realm, all that the people would become and do. But He saw beyond that and He has prepared even for times such as this. He has an answer. And, you know, even in the midst of our biggest failings, we're still *worth it* to Him. How wide and deep, vast and endless as the ocean of the Greater Archipelagos, that is His *love*. That is how enormous His heart is."

Iviana sat silently for a while, refusing to reveal her thoughts to those who waited. Even Darist's curious stare she avoided. She needed time to process all she had heard, for she had expected nothing like it.

At last, she stood and started for the door.

"Where are you going?" Chamaeleo asked, at a loss for the first time since Iviana had known her.

"The Great One created that realm with such... love, purity and honor... and I'm not going to let this perversion of His gift continue any longer."

Darist followed her to the door. "We're going to the Greater Archipelagos?" he asked.

"Are *we?*" she asked, somewhat surprised he meant to join her, even though he still knew little of what it was all about.

"Of course, *we* are."

Marquen walked through the door then and said, "I'm guessing we're going to wreak a little havoc?"

"Absolutely," Iviana replied.

"I'm coming too!" cried Era, who had remained silent for so long. When Iviana appeared surprised by her outburst, she said, "I did not come all this way to be left out."

Iviana took hold of her hands and said, "Of course, you must come. You're as much a part of this as I am."

"I wonder how you're planning on getting there," said Chamaeleo with an eyebrow raised.

"Oh, well, I suppose the door in Jaela's Cavern," said Iviana with new wonder at understanding the meaning behind the name.

"Well, if it helps, I brought along a few friends... a few flying friends," offered Chamaeleo, knowingly. "They or *he,* in particular, is waiting for you in the forest. Era will take you there."

"You're not coming with us?" asked Era.

"No. I've another errand to see to. But I will

meet you there, I think."

All of a sudden, Iviana noticed Merri sitting on the bed, wide-eyed and stunned.

"Oh, Merri..." Iviana's voice trailed off when Merri met her gaze, her face bright and alive.

"So all those stories you told about the Great One and the splendid land in another world..." muttered Merri, "...*the Greater Archipelagos*, where the people have extraordinary gifts bestowed by a wondrous Being... they were all true? And that is where you come from?"

Iviana nodded. "Well, where my parents were from."

Merri laughed with delight. "Wait until I tell the children!"

Darist tugged on Iviana's sleeve then. "What about Nimua and Necoli? I believe he wanted to show her around a nearby town. I can't say when they'll be back, but it won't be for some time."

Iviana debated on what to do, but knew she must move against her own desires, no matter how wrong it felt. "We cannot wait," she insisted regretfully. "We really haven't another moment to spare... I can feel it. Something is coming to a head." She turned to Merri then. "Will you tell them where we've gone?"

Merri nodded, looking on her as if she was an enchanted being. "Of course," she said solemnly.

With that, the four bid them farewell and Era led the others through the woods into a large clearing. When Iviana spotted Tragor there, in their old place—the place she had often wandered over the last few days, fearing she might never see him again—she flew toward him without another thought and wrapped her arms around him, nuzzling her cheek into his neck.

"You darling dragon, how is it you're always here when I need you? And why have you not come before now?"

She gazed into his eyes and found his character within them; she knew just where he'd been: flying over the cannibal island, doing his best to watch over the prisoners in her absence. Likely, he had not approved of her leaving any more than she herself had.

"I'm sorry I let you down. You believed in me, when first we met. I will do my best not to disappoint you again. What do you say we *free them*?"

His green eyes grew bright and were full of affection for more than her willingness to save the imprisoned. He loved the little lost girl he'd picked up in a wasteland, the one so like his Latos.

Iviana found Era standing awkwardly by and asked, "How did you know to bring the extra dragons?" She gestured to the two beside Tragor.

"We came prepared," Era said with a smile.

As Darist and Marquen pulled themselves atop the other two dragons, Iviana saw that Era was making ready to leap upon Tragor.

"Oh, dear, I don't know if he will take you," she said worriedly. "He doesn't like people."

Era looked at Tragor admiringly. "Oh, but we flew together. I believe we've become friends."

"Really?" Iviana asked Tragor. "I'm not the only woman in your life anymore, old boy?" She leaped upon him and pulled Era up behind her. With that, they took to the air, flying faster than any of them ever had before.

Iviana didn't exactly have all the details lined up—such as how they would keep from being killed and eaten or how they would get them all off the island—but she knew the Great One was with her and would supply. She could feel Him all around her, inside of her, pulsating through her veins, pumping through her heart, smiling into her spirit. All she must do was move, trust Him and all would come out as it must.

Knowing Darist and Marquen ought to know all, she filled them in while the dragons took a moment to rest. She knew Era must have known most of it, but to hear it again seemed to rock her.

"Thank you for letting me come," was all Darist was able to mutter in his low, almost threatening voice. It was apparent he was harboring indignation he did not yet know what to do with.

Marquen responded with great emotion. "I knew something was afoot, but the Great One never revealed it to me. I am ashamed I hid away on my mountain. I only did so because I thought if I stayed out of the council's business, I would not be considered a threat." He swallowed, as if attempting to hold back tears. Iviana had never seen him so affected. "I succeeded, but..."

"Marquen," Iviana interrupted. "It was the Great One's will that you lived in your hills, hidden away for another time. If He had wanted you to know before now, He would have *told* you. Take comfort in that you are one of the few in the Greater Archipelagos who shares a friendship with the Great One. Most everyone else is too awed or intimidated, too rebellious or closed-minded to give Him all He ever wanted: friendship... family."

Marquen offered a small smile, saying. "I think

our roles just exchanged, Chosen One."

Iviana ignored him. No matter what happened, Marquen was and always would be her greatest councilor aside from her Great Friend.

❧16❧

Flynn

STANDING BEFORE THE door, Flynn found he could not do what had been asked of him—or, rather, demanded. He was expected to program the door that led into Jaela's Cavern to deny his friends' re-entrance. Certainly, it would make them safer, for they would be in grave danger if they ever attempted to return, but there was a part of him that *wanted* them to return. They were his closest friends, his family. Iviana was...

Well, Iviana was, after all, the one who had brought him to this world to be its leader, if a cowardly, spineless one he was turning out to be. Besides, he could not deny she truly was his dearest friend, the one closest to his heart, the one he kicked himself every day for not defending in her hour of need, when she had been bold and courageous so often in his presence. If only she had rubbed off on him. If only she had been made Realm Leader in his stead. Perhaps she had made a mistake. But then, he had been anointed with agelessness. Surely, the Great One would not have done so had He not approved of the one filling the position. That was something he would never understand.

Flynn stared at the panel that awaited his touch, his command to seal his friends from this world forever, and took a step back. How could the council truly expect him to do this? Did they think him *that* spineless? Of course, if they did, it was his own doing. And certainly, if Iviana was as smart as he thought her, she would not return. But if she ever chose to do so, he would not deny her.

Never.

Brenna had spoken with him in secret the evening Iviana and the others had fled. They had discussed further the end of their engagement and Brenna had been able to wriggle a little out of him about the situation with Iviana, though not enough to put her in jeopardy. They had examined the months in which they had grown close and even pinpointed when things had begun to change—when the beginning of the end had taken place, though neither had wanted to acknowledge it. And then, of course, as it happened, he *had* been changing, as he knew Iviana had perceived. It was more than evident in the way she looked at him, in her tone, when she had spoken to him that last time.

No, there was no question of what to do. He would leave the door open to them. And perhaps, somehow, something could be done about...

Anyway, the council would never know if he had done what they'd asked. At least he had the wits to know that much.

"Greetings, young man," spoke a charming voice.

Flynn leaped about, but relaxed when he recognized Chamaeleo. "What brings you here?" he said in greeting. "Is there something I can do for you?"

"No. No, not for me."

"Then who?"

"A number of people. Namely yourself, I think."

"What is it?"

"I thought I'd let you know that Iviana is going to free the prisoners today."

"What?" Flynn almost jumped at the thought Iviana might be in the realm even then. "But how?"

"However she can, I suspect."

Flynn stood stock still, his mind racing.

"Well?" Chamaeleo urged. "Are you going to let her do it alone?"

Flynn looked up, feeling ultimately free for the first time in a long while. "Not a chance."

"Oh, I hoped you'd say that... You should also know I overheard what I believe is your council having the final vote on what is finally to be done with the prisoners in the mountain."

Flynn's demeanor darkened and he wondered how often they had had meetings behind his back. "And?"

"They chose to relinquish them to the cannibals... this evening, I believe."

Flynn paled as his stomach twisted, as if he might purge its contents. "If Iviana had not come..." he muttered as he took in the realization. He turned to Chamaeleo then, saying, "I must go." With that, he seemed to grow into his old self, with the addition of a little life experience, and started in the direction of the dragon's lair.

❧17❧

IVIANA

THE SIGHT OF the cannibal island as Iviana and the others soared over made her ill. She detested what was inside it, what secrets it held and, mostly, she hated its namesake... the fact that people who consumed their own kind dwelt within its landscape, with the permission of the council, no less. It had been an unkindness to allow the cannibals to live in their sickness. Even so, they would be her enemy should they discover her. Their charge was to guard the secret and they would do so by any means necessary. She prayed by some miracle they would get the innocent people away without anyone getting hurt.

At last, they landed upon the sparkling white coastline. Iviana couldn't help noticing the steam that rose from its granules. Placing her hand to them, they were hot to the touch. This had not been the case previously. It was as if the rays of the sun were magnified here and she contemplated why this would be. It was almost as if the sun had cast its eye upon this place in particular.

Once Era had wriggled down from Tragor's back, Iviana stole the moment to embrace him, to absorb whatever courage he could give her. She was suddenly fearful, certain she could not do this. But her dragon had guarded over the island in her absence and she would not let him or the Great One down, so she entreated them both for strength.

When Tragor drew back from her, he looked into her face, attempting to convey some message. Though she had, as of late, begun to read him keenly, she could not seem to understand him in that moment. There was too much else in her mind. Still, she knew he meant to leave her. For what purpose, she could not fathom.

"But I need you *here*," she told him, nearly sobbing, but checking herself that the others would not hear.

The great dragon shook his head about, not unlike a horse shaking flies from its mane. He then sent her a final, almost desperate look, trying doubly hard to assure her, but still she could not read it. All she knew was that she wanted him there with her. Even so, he lifted into the air and disappeared into the clouds.

Iviana felt terribly lost without him. But suddenly a hand was placed upon her back and she turned to find Era at her side. Somehow, though she hardly knew the girl, this comforted her. Era was a deeply kindred spirit and was offering her support.

Darist approached impatiently with, "Lets do this." It was obvious the shock of it all was pushing him forward. He could not stand by another moment with such knowledge.

Iviana wondered what he thought of her having lived with it so long.

Great One. Iviana closed her eyes and focused on the Creator of the world. *I need you now. I do not see a clear path. Come to me.*

Immediately, she felt herself enveloped by warmth that did not lessen as the seconds passed. Instead, it grew inside her, and she knew it would remain—knew, somehow, it had been there for some time before it had made itself known. It was all she needed now.

Her eyes fluttered open at a sort of pecking on her shoulder and there was the white spirit–dove. *I am with you... always,* the spirit of the Anointed One whispered. Those had been the first words he had ever spoken to her when she had been dangling from a chain over a great abyss. She had not known then from Whom the words had come, but she knew it now and knew them to be true. With that, the dove flew toward the glaring sun.

"Are you ready?" Marquen asked gently.

Iviana nodded. "Now, I am."

Leading them onto the path to the mountain's entrance, Iviana found the boulder that covered the entryway solidly tucked in place. She wracked her brain for a plan until Darist strutted over. He lifted the boulder as if it was a pebble and heartily tossed it over the edge of the cliff where it crumbled to pieces. His job done, Darist returned to them with eyebrows cockily raised, much like the Darist Iviana had known when first she had met him.

"Beautifully done, friend," she admitted with a grin.

Eyes sparkling with humor, he muttered, "Now, that's done..." and entered the cavern, but immediately took notice of their next problem.

They would need light.

"Oh, dear," Iviana muttered under her breath, searching her mind for a way to light their way. She had not brought the needed supplies to light a torch.

"Oh, you need light," said Marquen. With that, he snapped his fingers where a flame immediately sparked, balancing on his pointer finger.

"I suppose you're going to be telling us that's a Great Gift too?" Iviana asked, astonished.

"No, just a trick for company."

Iviana's brows raised. "Truly?"

He laughed. "Of course not. It *is* a gift, I expect, though I don't know any more about it."

"Light-bringer… Light-bearer?" Era suggested.

"Fancy," Darist commented.

"Well, what else can you do with it?" Iviana asked.

"I really couldn't say. I found it by accident. Haven't had the chance to use it often."

Iviana studied the flame, purple in hue, not unlike the color the light her healing power created. "We should definitely look into that," she said as they entered the tunnels.

When Iviana found the tunnel system too complicated for her memory, she resorted to her Seeker's fire. It was not long after that she noticed Era seemed to know the way and asked if she'd memorized it when she'd followed her in her dream.

"Oh, no, I'm terrible with directions," she

admitted. "I'm a Seeker."

Iviana halted and turned to her. "Truly? I thought I was the only one?"

Era nodded. "I know. When it came time for the new Realm Leader to be found, they thought they would have to send me above, but then you turned up."

"So... you can move through time *and* you're one of two Seeker's in the realm?"

"I guess I'm a Dream-walker, too, so Chamaeleo says."

Iviana smiled in astonishment. "Glad to have you along."

"She almost makes you and Marquen seem normal," Darist added.

"Almost?" Iviana queried with a raised brow.

Marquen cleared his throat. "Not to rush things, but I believe we have a serious mission to complete. If you could find it possible to walk and talk at the same time...?"

With that, the Seekers started forward until whispers sounded up ahead, followed by moans and coughing.

"It's them, isn't it?" Era asked.

Iviana noted her face was pale, as if frightened to face the tragedy ahead, but she took hold of Era's hand and gave it a squeeze. "We're here to rescue them. They aren't going to be here much longer."

Era nodded and her face gained color, but the sadness in her eyes did not diminish.

At last, they came to the opening in the large cavern where hundreds of the Greater Archipelagos' people were stowed away. *How have they lived all this time?* Iviana wondered. *By eating from the scraps the cannibals provided... scraps to feed hundreds?* They had to be starving, not to mention sickly. Yet, they lived. Iviana could only hope none had perished in this wretched place... that they would live to see the light of day.

The sound of their footfalls drew the attention of the prisoners and, after some mumbling and shoving about, Waymith and his daughter Jaela were produced, along with Shynn and her husband Japha.

"Oh, I am so glad to see you alive and well," called Shynn as Iviana approached. "We have been so afraid you might have put yourself in danger."

"But what are you doing here, child?" Waymith asked. "Why have you returned and endangered the lives of those who accompany you?"

"Hush, now," Iviana comforted. "We're here to free you."

"The council agreed to let us go?" Waymith

asked hopefully. "How did you do it?"

"No... I'm afraid it's just us—us and the Great One." When his face dropped, she asked the small group, "Will you trust me? Trust *Him*?"

The four looked to one another, then turned to those who had been listening nearby.

Eventually, Jaela came back with, "We will trust the Great One and the one He has chosen. What is your plan?"

That was a very good question.

Iviana's hands fell on the bars and she shook them, testing their strength. They were rock solid. She then approached the nearest door and found it was made of the same material as the bars, but this would be the most vulnerable place, if any.

"Darist," she called.

"Right here," he said from behind her. "Waiting... patiently."

Iviana smiled and stepped aside.

Darist approached then, took hold of the handle and turned, planning to force it open, but quickly pulled his hand away. "That's odd."

"What is it?" Iviana asked nervously.

He proceeded to shake at the door and then at the bars, but nothing would budge under his anointed strength.

"Ivi, I don't understand it. I've never encountered anything like this before. Unless..." He suddenly lifted Iviana as if she were a feather. "Never-mind. I still have my gift."

One of the prisoners spoke up. "We believe they were created to withstand the Great Gifts."

"That Inventor sounds familiar," Era said bitterly.

"You know him?" asked Iviana

"Not personally, but I'll bet you this Inventor is the one who creates Kurnin's Elixir." Then she added with a whisper, "The one that removes people's gifts."

Iviana nodded. "We'll do our best to see that never happens."

"Well, what do we do now?" Darist asked. It was obvious he was angered by his lack of aid.

Iviana turned to Marquen. "What do you think?"

Marquen had a ready answer. "I think we should pray."

Iviana returned to where Waymith and the others were. "We've hit a snag. Can you rally everyone to intercede for an answer?"

Jaela's eyes dimmed, as if she had already begun to lose hope, but she turned to shout to the prisoners, "Pray for a way, my brothers and sisters. If ever we are to be freed from this mountain, this is the day."

"If only they knew how many times we've done this," shouted a man from somewhere among them.

"They think they know what they're doing because they're not in here," someone said bitterly. "Just wait until they're caught. They'll understand we're not a bunch of fools."

"Please," Iviana called. "The Great One has sent us here Himself. He has done much to see that we followed through on His plans. He has a way. We have only to find it."

With that, the complaining ceased and the desperate murmuring of intercession filled the room.

Iviana turned from them and attempted to join, but found the glorious warmth that the Great One had stirred within her distracting. It was still growing in strength and, at times, felt as if it was sparking beneath her skin. These little pricks caught her off guard.

She closed her arms around herself in an attempt to block it out and cried to the Great One for an answer. But as she did so, the warmth lost its electric heat and transformed into something else entirely. Iviana could not say just what, but it was certainly a peculiar feeling, like heavy water poured out over and over, so much so her head physically moved in time. Those with her began to send her wondering glances, but she would not reject whatever was happening. Likely, it had its purpose.

"Your sword!" Era shouted.

Iviana looked down at it, but it appeared as it always did. "What of it?"

"It is said your blade cut through the bars that imprisoned our Realm Leader when you defeated Aradia," she explained.

Iviana stared down at it again. She had always wondered how it had done so... supposed she would never know. Even so, could it work in the same way again? This seemed her only answer. Pulling it from its sheath, she moved toward the bars and asked the prisoners to stay back. They looked her over skeptically, but did as she asked.

Gripping the weapon like a club, she swung it toward the bars and watched in amazement as the steel sliced through them like butter. Iviana stood back and glared at her blade. Twice, it had done the impossible and she wished she knew from where her mentor had obtained it.

Iviana turned to Era and embraced her tightly. "You're a genius!" she cried.

Pulling away, she saw that Era's eyes sparkled with a wide grin she could not quite conceal.

"Did any of you see that?" Iviana asked the prisoners.

A number of them nodded.

"Then you know the Great One has prepared your escape this day. Will you trust me from here on out?"

As news of what the sword had managed to do spread through their numbers, there were shouts of exaltation to the Great One. All at once, the people began stampeding to where the bars had been sliced, either to attempt escape or to see the miracle for themselves, but Iviana feared they would harm one another and called for them to cease, promising she would get them all out safely if they would be patient and follow her direction.

Iviana and those who had come with her worked to configure the best plan to get every person out safely. From there, Iviana reported to the crowd what they were to do and everyone took their positions. Era and Darist were at the mouth of the cavern, awaiting the first group they would lead out of the tunnel system. Luckily, the torches on the walls of the chamber were available to light their path. Era's Seeker's fire would direct them and

Darist's strength would be their best protection should they meet with danger.

To avoid this, the people were asked to move as silently as possible to keep from being heard in the passages. Iviana almost hoped for the cannibals' sake they would not be discovered, for they would surely find themselves stampeded by a great number of angry ex-prisoners.

Iviana cut away several of the other bars to create a larger exit that one to two people could pass through safely at a time. She made it no bigger, avoiding the chaos of hundreds of prisoners who were desperate to be free. Then, she and Marquen stood on either side of the exit to make certain things were kept in order. At last, they allowed the people to pass through one group at a time in order to avoid greater noise within the echoing chambers.

As each person passed, many stopped to embrace Iviana and Marquen and others cried their thanks as tears streamed down their faces. The two received this good-naturedly, but reminded them time was of the essence. The people did not have to be told twice.

❧18❧

IVIANA

WHEN AT LAST only a couple groups remained, awaiting Era and Darist's return, Iviana heard footsteps draw near and told the next group to be ready. However, when the person whom she had heard entered the room, her breath was stolen from her by the realization of who it was that raced toward her.

"Flynn!" she cried. "What are you doing here? You're not going to stop us—"

"No, no, please. I hate that you must think that. Chamaeleo informed me of what you were doing. I came as fast as I could. I'm here to help in any way I can. I will never be able to tell you how much I regret—"

Iviana cut him off to send the next group

through when Darist and Era arrived, so Flynn was forced to wait. While he waited, he studied the pale, sunken, sickly faces of those who passed by, those who had been imprisoned by *his* council, those he himself had forsaken. Iviana watched as he slowly sank to his knees and begged the Great One's forgiveness, penitent tears streaming down his face.

Iviana lifted him to his feet, if only to keep him from being trampled by the next group—the last.

"Iviana, can you ever forgive me?" he asked. "Will *they* ever be able to—"

"Flynn. I cannot convey how utterly elated I am you are here, ready and willing to do what is right, but right now, we must see this through. Then, we can talk."

Flynn nodded and his demeanor transformed from anguish to formidable determination. "What can I do?"

Iviana opened her mouth to give him a task, some place in their rescue, but could offer none. "I'm afraid we have it under control. This is the last group."

Without warning, Era ran into the cavern and screamed to Iviana that those outside had been spotted and the cannibals would be on their way.

"All right, everyone," she said to those left,

namely Jaela, Waymith, Shynn and Japha. "Never mind what noise you make, follow me!"

With that, they sprinted through the tunnels and down the mountain until they had met the others. Iviana knew their strength would be in numbers if it came to battle, but she also discerned the people were weak from starvation. Her mind raced for a better option.

"I will try speaking with them..." Iviana insisted as she faced Darist, Era and Marquen, "...try talking them down. But if they will not relent..."

"We may be half-starved," said Japha, having overheard, "but we have fury enough. We will crush these cannibals under our feet."

A number of the freed heard this as well and cheered their agreement. But Iviana could not stand the thought of bloodshed. The cannibals not only had health and experience, but they possessed actual weapons. Her blade would not go far, even if she wished to use it.

But the cannibals were drawing closer.

Iviana watched as their numbers raced toward the defenseless lot they had been abusing for years. How could they do such a thing? Then again, why would they not? They ate the flesh of their brothers. Imprisoning people had been nothing to them and killing would mean no more.

Unexpectedly, a great rumbling began to shake the surface of the island. The people's battle-cry died away and the cannibals ceased their chase as a thunderous roar sounded over the land. Those upon the island searched for the source until all eyes fell upon the very mountain that had served as a prison as it crumbled from its very foundation.

Iviana's mind raced. How was this occurring?

With a jolt, the answer came to her.

"Flynn," she whispered hoarsely. "Flynn?!" she shrieked. "Where's Flynn?"

"That young man who was crying in the mountain?" asked Shynn. "He did not follow us out. I'm not certain what he was about, but..." She followed Iviana's gaze to the mountain.

Iviana grew horrified as the mountain continued to disintegrate before them. She knew exactly what Flynn was doing. He was using his Speaker's gift to destroy the corrupt dungeon once and for all. "He's calling down the mountain!" she cried aloud. "He's using his gift to destroy it! Oh, Flynn!" she sobbed.

With that, she raced toward it. She must get him out before he was destroyed by his own deed. She must see him again, speak to him, tell him what her heart had only recently uncovered. No matter what he had done or how much shame he carried, he could not die this way—not before...

Hands flew around her waist, pulling her back with exceptional force.

"Darist, let me go! Flynn is in there! We have to get him out!"

He ignored her and the two watched as the mountain concluded its transformation into a pile of rocks.

"Flynn!" Iviana screamed through her tears. *"Oh, Flynn!"* How could he do this? She understood his conviction, the remorse he must have suffered, but there was yet absolution.

She turned to Darist and beat at his chest before looking up into his face, hot tears streaming down her cheeks, at an utter loss for what to do.

"Flynn did... what he thought best," he said slowly, obviously trying to hold it together for her sake. "He destroyed the very thing that had been used to hurt his people. It can never be utilized for such purposes again. But right now, we've got a whole lot of half-mad people about to enter into battle. They need *you*."

Iviana could not remove her eyes from the face of her friend, fearful she would lose her hold on reality if she confronted the chaos around her, the loss...

In that moment, the power the Great One had bestowed upon her when she'd landed on the island was yet rolling and toiling within. It reached into her heart and mind and offered her yet more of its strength. She grasped at it and fed for as long as she could stand. Though it was heavy and, oh, so unearthly, it was enough to pull her together.

"Look," Darist gasped, glancing at the sky above.

Iviana followed his gaze and her heart was warmed by what she saw until she realized the handful of dragons landing upon the island were not alone. They had riders.

Iviana raced to the head dragon who carried two familiar faces: Kurnin and Naii. Her stomach twisted when, at her approach, Kurnin yanked the woman down from the dragon's back and demanded Iviana remain where she was.

"Using her for a shield, Kurnin?" Iviana asked in a low voice.

"Nothing wrong with a little security," he said easily.

Iviana turned her attention to Naii, looking her over for signs of harm. "Naii," she said with great relief to find her well and whole. "How have you fared?"

Naii produced a restrained smile. "It's been... political."

"What in the world have you done with my mountain?" Kurnin asked with mild irritation, as if scarcely impressed by the sight.

"It got what you deserve, Kurnin. But then, as I've tried to tell you, another has paid the price for your iniquities. I suppose he's the only one who can save you now."

"From *what?* A little girl and her army of sallow offenders? I'm fairly certain we can handle it."

"On the contrary, a girl, her army of Chosen Ones and the Great One Himself. You have no idea how invested He is in this—no idea what you've set yourself up against."

"Still think you're special, do you? You think He wants people like these running around with the capacity to harm His realm?"

"He lets *you* run free, doesn't he?"

Kurnin grinned at that. "I'm flattered, truly. Obviously, you think more of me than I realized. If I'm such a danger, what do you say we simply talk this matter over and end things peacefully."

Iviana raised her brows. "Perfect. I'm going to need dragons—lots of dragons. And I'll need homes for the homeless along with clothes and food supplies. I want these people to have all the comforts they've gone without as soon as possible."

Kurnin studied her for a moment before he burst with laughter, bending over and resting his hands on his knees for support. "Oh, I should have known you would not be sensible," he said laughingly. "You *are* very funny, though."

He then turned and called to the head of the cannibal tribe. "They're all yours, as we discussed. I'll even throw in the extras. Though I warn you..." He gestured to Iviana. "...she's a handful."

"No," Iviana pleaded. "How can you think of doing such a thing? You know what they are capable of!"

Abruptly, a noise not unlike the crumbling of the mountain cut off her speech, but upon searching the island's landscape, there was nothing to be found.

"What are you doing now?" Kurnin accused, for the first time appearing mildly anxious.

Iviana did not correct him. Let him think it was her, that she was capable of such a thing. She had split the earth open once before, in any case. Perhaps it was doing so now.

As people began to point to something over the ocean, Iviana's attention was drawn to where a portion of the water bubbled fiercely, hurling frenzied waves from its center. Whatever was below was enormous and Iviana couldn't help wondering if it would be a danger to those on the island. Or might it possibly be a help, working as a distraction while she gathered a plan to rescue her people?

Startlingly, what was producing the display broke the ocean's surface, shooting an almost tangible pulse in every direction, as if whatever was being uncovered held great power over that region in a realm unseen. Iviana grew to understand this as she looked on in wonder, for the transparent dome of the lost Isle of Atlantyss ascended in glittering splendor, lit brilliantly by the pronounced rays of the illuminating sun.

"*Atlantyss!*" Era cried ecstatically from somewhere in the crowd behind her.

It was a marvelous sight to behold, but its meaning struck Iviana full force. The Great One was raising the Atlantians at this particular moment... for *this* hour. He was ready for their release into the world and that meant the world was prepared for them.

Currently, that seemed farthest from the truth.

The higher the domed city rose, the more furiously it sent waves toward the cannibal island.

Before long, those upon the shore were forced to race further inland as a mighty wave came generously rushing toward them, soon smashing with a vengeance over the coast, giving way to a sudden, unnerving calm as Atlantyss settled into place.

At last, the ocean growing tranquil, the glistening dome that had protected the island for so long began to descend, unveiling the glory of that great city. Vibrant flags waved from spires that jetted heavenward, adorning the towering architecture that had been constructed in various distinctive hues. Above these, soared buzzing nelepyres and elegant dragons, eager to be unleashed into the wide-open firmament beyond the dome. The plethora of people outfitted in foreign fashions moved animatedly and with purpose, clearly anticipating the prospects before them now they were no longer concealed. It was like peering into another world—a realm that presented wholly abandoned, unimpeded possibilities. The sight was fantastical, yet the true treasure was to be found in Atlantyss' passion and culture.

"That girl claimed it Atlantyss? Is this true?" Kurnin demanded of Iviana.

She nodded.

"Where have they come from? What have they

done? What is all of that?"

"The future, if I have anything to say about it," Iviana assured. "They've been hidden away at the bottom of the ocean since before Latos' death, that they could become all the Great One desired in perfect freedom, without you and your council butting in and removing the Great One's mantle from them."

Kurnin physically cringed with disgust at her speech. "How *dare* they?" he fumed.

Iviana was speechless. This was his response to that glorious city? Contempt?

"Never mind the spectacle, everyone," he shouted. "We'll handle that monstrosity soon. Just now, we must deal with the prisoners. They cannot leave this island, no matter the cost."

To Iviana's enthused delight, those on the Atlantian dragons and nelepyres started for their island as if in response to his words and soon joined them on the beach. They had recognized their trouble and had come to her aid even in what should have been their finest hour.

Thankfully, Kurnin stood stock still, finally paralyzed in his astonishment.

Probably stunned they would actually dare to enter his presence, thought Iviana. Still, she hoped this would show him he could no longer succeed. Atlantyss would be too much for them.

Nevertheless, he would not yield. He had a planet to maintain. "Call in the Enforcers," he shouted. At his command, a number of the council ascended on the backs of their dragons and disappeared into a large cloud.

Iviana was filled with foreboding while at the same moment drawn back to what was occurring inside her. It was now sending tremors through her body that she struggled to conceal from her enemy; she did not wish to appear weak. But it would not be hidden. It was unhinging.

Her attention was diverted from her plight as a vast cloud of dragons soared from their hiding place, their riders dressed in perfect, incandescent white. Iviana would have thought the spectacle grand had she not watched Kurnin's face contort into a monstrous grin, surveying his finest creation unveiled at last. These were the Enforcers. Seeing their numbers, their youth and the capacity for cruelty painted in their expressions, Iviana was pained that this should be their destiny.

Kurnin drew near her and spoke in a tone she had not heard from him before, "Iviana, I mean no harm. I love this world and I admire what Latos accomplished. I wish only to keep hold of his vision, to maintain the order and unity we have had since his reign. Surely, as his granddaughter, you can find it within yourself to understand that."

Iviana was so stunned by his speech, she could not easily find words with which to respond. Not to mention, she did not feel at all herself, twitching with power. Still, she stood her ground.

"Kurnin... *oh*, Kurnin, Latos never meant for any of this." She gestured to the prisoners, the cannibals and the Enforcers. "He believed in order and unity, yes, that this world might live in harmony, without war. But he stood for love and freedom, as well, and I think he would have appreciated the profusion of gifts the Great One has bestowed on our people, just as he would have enjoyed anything given from the hands of his Great Friend."

Kurnin shook his head. "I was wrong," he said. "How can you understand what a great man such as your grandfather desired for this realm, what he worked his whole life to accomplish? You did not know him and only learned of him recently. I have spent the whole of my life researching his great reign, so how dare you attempt to convince me—convince these people—that you know what his intentions were, that you know better than myself and this council his vision.

"You are and always have been a poison to this realm. It is time we remedied that." Turning to the Enforcers, he commanded, "Take them, take them all, but begin with *her*."

"I spoke that mountain into a pile of rocks," an astonishing voice with forceful conviction began, "and I'll do the same to any who touch this woman."

Iviana spun to face Flynn, nearly buckling but for the baffling substance that filled her.

"I am no longer afraid to do what *must* be done, if I have to," he continued. "In fact, I'll be spending the rest of my life righting the wrongs we have committed here, my council."

"Oh, don't take so much credit," scoffed Kurnin. "You were nothing more than a pebble to be kicked aside in our plans. If you persist in standing against us, we will be forced to replace you."

"Very well," Flynn replied readily. "As it should be. I was no leader, in any case."

Iviana longed to follow the dispute that continued, but could only be thankful Flynn was distracting them long enough for her to deal with the turmoil within. Even seeing Flynn alive had not been enough to draw her from whatever was taking place inside, for it was overpowering and her body trembled with it.

"Ivi... you all right?" Darist asked, placing a hand on her back.

Immediately, he withdrew it, eyes wide with concern.

It was only then Iviana realized her trembling was beginning to translate into the earth beneath her feet, much like it had the night she and Tragor had defeated Aradia in her underground lair. Then, the earth above had parted to reveal the starry night sky. This time, however, it felt as though she herself would split apart, as if every particle of her being might burst into a million pieces. This toiling thing which she had mistaken for a hearty supply of strength and courage had mutated into something *dangerous*. With all her might, she stood her ground, attempting to reign it in, to keep herself from exploding.

Even so, as the great gathering of people began to take notice, the power was only just beginning to have its way with her. Piercing beams shot forth from her eyes so all she could see was bright white light. But with that light came stillness and silence—not of the ground or the people, but of her own heart and mind. For within that light was a presence she knew well and He smiled upon her, inside of her spirit, *laughing* with delight. In that dazzling stillness, she was in the presence of the One she had yearned for more than anything in all the world.

And with that realization, her heart... fractured.

It was not painful nor did she fear it. As it continued to rupture, she released a guttural cry from the very depths of her soul until her heart *burst*—wide open and into dozens of tiny pieces, releasing the One Who had been contained there, the One Who, through her silent, growing longing, she'd invited to dwell there until He was all-consuming...until He simply could not be contained.

As the pieces of her heart drew together again, they were intermingled with that great power. From there, it flowed through her body until it found her arms where it collected until they were itching with the desire to move. All around, gasps could be heard as tangible glory streamed out from them in luminous strands of rich teal and shimmering gold, winding and curling about her.

Eyes parted and lips curled into a smile, Iviana moved her arms this way and that, watching the blue–gold glory swirl around them. Then, quite suddenly, she began to laugh a lovely, inviting, unrestrained utterance, anticipating what was to happen next, though she had no idea what it would be.

She was aware, in the back of her mind, Darist, Marquen, Era and Flynn were working to ease the people, for they were certain Iviana had come unhinged, or that, perhaps, she was working in the same dark arts Aradia had. Even those Iviana had freed were growing suspicious.

"What is that depraved girl doing *now*?" Kurnin cried, horrified. "Stop her!" he commanded of Iviana's friends. "Stop her, now!" It was apparent he was by no means willing to draw near her himself.

Nevertheless, Iviana was centered with the Great One and knew from Whom the unnerving substance came, reveling in the knowledge as her blood quickened and sparked and her heart pulsed in chorus with what was to come.

At last, obeying the power's desperate urging, she thrust her arms outward. Instantly, a great, gushing river of dazzling, glorious teal-gold water burst forth from them. The supernatural liquid devastated all in its wake, sending cannibals, councilmen, Enforcers, Atlantians and ex-prisoners soaring through the air. Screams sounded from those who had fled in time, scrambling for dear life. But those who had been captured unprepared continued to be tossed about in the devastation.

The sensation was almost too much for Iviana; it was utterly engrossing, consuming and liberating at once. All she had felt before had been but a prelude to the moments that now passed. She was totally and utterly undone. For all she knew, her skin had been ripped from her and her spirit was pouring out, or rather scattering and bursting into the atmosphere. There was no going back and there was no escape; there was not even alleviation or comfort. She had only to stand as a threshold for the fluid from another, far superior realm, from the very kingdom of the Great One.

The force of the formidable substance was searing a great trench through the earth where a tangible river formed. Those who had been unable to escape the shimmering torrent—that was beginning to ease now it had found its home—were filled with incredulity as they found ailments healed and looked wonderingly at restored limbs and reset bones, at vanishing cuts, soars and aches. Those who could not speak, hear, see or walk were doing all of these and laughing with joyous elation at the realization.

It wasn't long before those who had fled prior

observed this and crept back, the bravest diving or wading into the river that had now slowed to a steady, satisfying rhythm, where they began to receive visions, heart healings and were given new destinies. It was then the laughing, dancing and frolicking began to unleash as a people who had previously been terrified were becoming undone in their own right. Those who had begun as enemies instantly and miraculously became comrades and sadness and anger transformed into ecstasy and tenderness as they were covered and filled by the qualities within the divine flow.

To Iviana's astonishment, she glimpsed Kurnin and the council swimming and playing in the glory-water. Flynn was beside Kurnin as they shared wide grins and *splashed* one another like children. Despite her current condition and all she barely understood, this was more than she could have hoped for: to see Kurnin and the others letting go and relenting to the mysterious work of the unearthly river. Though, she doubted they could have helped it. They had been among the first to have been furiously swept up by the initial wave and this water was by no means ordinary water, containing qualities of a realm they did not know or understand that produced highly peculiar effects on all it touched. Likewise, this was no ordinary revolution; it was the kind of encounter you never came back from.

At long last, the beating tide within Iviana was spent. Dropping her arms, she struggled to remain upright, for she had been used as the Great One's vessel like none other. Finally, she fell into the water where Darist, Marquen, Flynn and Era carefully lifted her onto the riverbank.

∽19∾

ᴛᴠɪᴀɴᴀ

ᴛᴠɪᴀɴᴀ ᴀᴡᴏᴋᴇ ᴛᴏ the sound of ringing laughter. Without moving, she opened her eyes. It had come from a group made up of Flynn, Kurnin, Naii, Waymith, Jaela and the rest of the council. To her pleasure, they were chatting as freely as children, their eyes aglow with youth.

Casting her gaze elsewhere, she was shocked to find most everyone who had previously been there were gone. Either they had moved to another part of the island or they had been taken elsewhere. Seeing how happy the group was, she could safely assume everything had ended peaceably.

It pleased her to see the few others who remained were yet enjoying the supernatural river's company. A couple of young women sat on the riverbank, soaking their feet and gazing dreamily into its depths. Others swam contentedly on their backs, staring up at the glory of the orange and pink sky painted by the sun's departing rays. Others simply sat nearby, conversing in small groups and often pointing to the water as if sharing stories.

Iviana sat up and found Era sleeping beside her. She comprehended the girl had not wished to leave her on her own and had given up merry-making with the others to guard her. If this was so, Iviana was profoundly touched.

Seeing Marquen headed in her direction and not wanting to wake Era, she slowly stood and met him halfway.

"The Glory-bringer has awoken," he said with a wry grin.

"Since when did you take up teasing?" she asked.

He thought a moment, as if this had not occurred to him. "I would gather since I left my hill and began spending time with your friends. You're all terribly sarcastic. I'm afraid it's catching. Besides, I wasn't entirely joking. That is the name the prophesies gave you and it is what you have become. I have much to write about after today."

Iviana took his words to heart. Glory-bringer? She would never own that grand title, to be sure…

but it *was* what she had been used to do. The Great One had used her to rescue this world in His utterly mystifying performance and had apparently been planning to do so since long before she was born. She may never understand why He had chosen her and perhaps there was no special reason. But she was grateful He had had a plan... that He had seen what was to come and she had answered His call, else the future Era had seen would have come upon them sooner than she had realized.

Brushing these thoughts away for another time, she asked, "Where has everyone gone?"

"Well, the reformed cannibals returned to their village for celebrating. Though, as you see, a few have remained beside the river. I do not blame them."

"*Fully* reformed?"

He nodded. "The river worked its magic on everyone."

"Where is everyone else?"

"You should have seen it. Just as we were attempting to make plans, Tragor flew in with a great multitude of dragons—more than we ever knew existed, proving there are definitely other lairs in our world—providing transportation for all who needed it. At any rate, Flynn, Kurnin, Naii and Shynn worked to organize where they could be taken for the time being. Some were simply sent to Atlantyss, others to various nearby islands including the Isle of Dragons. Some even opted to remain here. It went remarkably smooth, I have to say."

"*Tragor*, that wonder," she gasped. "I should have known. Where is he now?"

Marquen pointed to a green and blue dragon lazing on the far beach. Iviana was immediately drawn that way, but Darist called to her before she could get far.

"Iviana," he said as he approached, his eyes sparkling with glee.

"What is it?"

"It's just... I have some people you need to meet." He gestured to Shynn and Japha, whom she had not even been aware were yet on the island.

"Oh, I know them, Darist. Didn't you see me speaking with them before?"

"But we have only just discovered something," Shynn put in warmly.

"All right, I'm listening," relented Iviana, though she was utterly exhausted.

"Well... you see, as it turns out... we have just discovered you are our *niece*."

Iviana could not move, could not even remove

her eyes from the woman. Could it be true? She had family? *Real* family? "But I was told there was no one left," she squeaked.

"I suppose that is because they did not want you to know, those who knew we were yet alive, that is. The council had not approved of our being missionaries, but there was nothing they could do to stop us as the right to be ministers to other worlds had been instated in the time of Latos. At any rate, they had, as much as they could, disowned us. We had been away from the Greater Archipelagos for so many years they probably had not expected us to ever return. I don't suppose our circumstances worked in your favor any more than your parents' did. After all, we left to do our work even before they left."

Iviana blinked at them a few times, looking between the two—*her* aunt and uncle. Then she flew into Shynn's arms and hugged her tightly. Japha wrapped his large arms around the two.

Drawing back, Shynn said, "But there is more... I understand you know our son Necoli."

This time, Iviana truly was caught up in the wonderment of it all. "Your... your son... Necoli? But he said... I mean he thought you were... dead."

Shynn shook her head. "No, though I can

rightly understand why he assumed us killed by the cannibals."

Iviana laughed. "He will be so elated, you have no idea! How wonderful! Wait, this means Necoli is my *cousin.*"

"But there is yet *more...*" Shynn continued hesitantly.

Iviana waited, uncertain what more there could possibly be.

"Necoli is technically not our son, though he does not know it. We raised him from birth and we love him as if he truly was our own. But, you see, he is our nephew and my brother Redden's child."

This time, Iviana was truly speechless. Redden was *her* father.

She looked to Darist, who appeared just as surprised as she at this news.

Iviana swallowed. "You mean...?"

Shynn nodded, tears filling her eyes. "He is your twin. It seems you were left with Naphtali and he with us. We were not even told about you, I swear it, or we would gladly have made you our own as well. How I wish you would have been..."

Iviana's mind raced with questions. Oh, how could they all be answered?

"I can only suppose they did not want to feel

they were putting too large a burden on anyone, so you were left with Naphtali instead. I suppose she never mentioned you had a brother?"

"No," Iviana replied. And she knew her Naphtali had not known of his existence. She had kept many things from her, but this she would never have kept secret; it was too important. Iviana wished she knew why her parents had not kept them, but this day had been too full and that was a question for another day, one on which, perhaps, she had her new-found brother by her side.

Suddenly, a pair of arms scooped around her from behind and squeezed tightly.

"Flynn, let me breathe!" she gasped.

He laughingly released her and turned her about to face him. "I'm so glad you're awake, Ivi. I've been waiting and waiting, but Darist wouldn't let me bother you. We've got to tell you of all we have planned, all the changes and the—"

"That's all very well, Flynn, and I'm terribly sorry to put you off, but I think if I learn anything else this day, I'll burst. Wait until I've had some sleep, won't you?"

Obviously disappointed, he covered it with a large smile that was very like his former self. Even so, it was clear he had gained in strength and dignity.

Even the way he carried himself and the way he spoke when he turned to those who had approached with him showed he would make a true leader thereafter. Iviana could not help feeling the utter relief of it.

"If you'll allow me to interrupt," said Kurnin, standing before Iviana. "I... would like to apologize to you, Glory-bringer... and to *thank you*." He hung his head a moment, but then raised it. "I am a changed man, I assure you. I wish nothing but to see this land prosper in the way you have shown us today. I—I cannot bear facing what we might have lost had you not—"

"Oh, please, don't thank me. You think I knew how to do that? Granted, it may have come through me, but I could not have accomplished it on my own."

Kurnin bowed his head to show his understanding, but met her gaze again. "I thank you... because you *defied* me—us—on every level. We needed it, *clearly*."

"Please," stepped in Grandia, "consider his sentiments ours." She gestured to the rest of the council, who offered Iviana subtle bows.

"And I must thank you, as well," said a man Iviana vaguely remembered. Seeing her confusion, he added, "I am Loloi, the head of this island, a people who shall be forever changed by the gift you bestowed upon us: *freedom* from our iniquity. You will be remembered for as long as this island is in existence."

All of this was terribly uncomfortable for Iviana. Obviously, these people saw her as some grand being, but she was still *her*. Flynn and Darist made it clear they enjoyed the spectacle of her discomfort as they stood smirking and elbowing one another. How she wished Nimua was there to read her mind and smuggle her away. Even so, she was eternally grateful to hear the promises of change and a better life.

"I am glad," she interrupted Loloi. "I am so glad the Great One did such marvelous work. I am grateful for your own sakes and for the Greater Archipelagos. Seeing you all before me, transformed and shining, you are remarkably beautiful —beautiful, especially, to the One who created you and affected you this day. Please, extend any further thanks to *Him*... for I must go." She turned to Flynn and Darist and added, "Tragor and I will go to the Isle of Dragons. I'll meet you there."

With that, she turned from them and made her way in the direction of the shoreline. But coming upon the banks of the river of glory, she stopped and stared down at the water. Peering down the river's way, she found it stretched clear to the end of the island and flowed into the sea, but it was evident by the unnatural current it was not receiving any of the ocean water and, therefore, would not be diluted.

Slowly, she stepped into the river and noticed at once the peculiar sensations it sent through her, tingling under her skin as it had when it had been waiting and building inside her, though this version was much milder. Seeing those floating about and soaking their feet, she doubted it affected them this way. They appeared peaceful, but she felt strange and exhilarated, as if filled with lightning. Swiftly, she splashed across and leaped from its depths onto dry land.

She then turned and peered into it again, taking note of its silky consistency, not quite water, but not quite *not* water. It sparkled and shimmered like no other liquid she had ever seen and seemed to *sing* as the wind blew through. It was utterly impossible and magnificent at once. She could scarcely believe it was truly there—that it is had come through *her*—could not quite believe it had revolutionized a people and would transform the whole world, if she had anything to say about it.

At last, she drew away, searching the beach to

find Tragor with Era, who was rubbing his face as if he was a pet... a very pampered pet. Iviana had never thought of him this way and might never have treated him so, but he certainly did not seem to mind it from Era. Iviana was glad he had opened his heart to another.

"My, how he likes you," she commented as she approached. Raising her arm to touch his sleek green face, she was cut short.

"I want to come with you," Era informed fervently.

"Of course, you can ride back with us. Tragor and I wouldn't have it any other way."

"No, not just there."

Iviana was taken aback. "Well... where would you like to go? Oh, back to Atlantyss, I suppose?"

Era shook her head. "You're going to travel."

Iviana thought a moment and realized this was so. "Yes. I am. But how did you know?"

"Oh, how I long to go, Iviana. *Please*, bring me with you!" Era was desperate, obviously near tears.

Iviana did not understand her desperation, but she knew what her answer would be. "Era, you are a remarkable young woman and have proved yourself a worthy friend this day. Unquestionably, you can come. In fact, I would dearly *like* to have your company." She stopped to study the face before her and was confused by what she discovered. "I cannot say just why, but I feel quite familiar with you. We've only known one another less than a day."

Era returned her gaze with an expression that understood something Iviana did not. "We'll have time enough to catch up," she promised.

❧20❧

Iviana

"I HAVE SOMETHING I need to ask you," Flynn said, taking a seat at Iviana's kitchen table.

Flynn's visit was unexpected since his meeting with his current council members was supposed to have gone much longer. There were so many things for them to discuss. The foremost thing on *Iviana's* mind was seeing Flynn's proposal of adding the Atlantian Island Leaders, Ferrol, Jephran and Mae, to his council. If the Atlantian culture was to affect the whole realm, that would be the best and fastest course of action, not to mention they were trustworthy and forward-thinking people.

"Not until you tell me what I want to know," she replied.

"Of course the council accepted them. It was only myself, Naii and a few others. You may, however, be surprised to hear I'll be moving to Atlantyss soon."

Iviana looked up at him. "Seriously?"

He nodded. "They are the future of our world and it was agreed the Realm Leader should be at the center of it. Therefore, Atlantyss is the new capital island."

"New capital island?" she asked in her astonishment. "How open-minded of you all."

"Well, we've had quite a lot of changes around here, if you hadn't noticed, 'Glory-bringer.'"

Iviana scowled. "Don't you dare call me that."

"And why not? You did a thing none of us ever dreamed could occur and most of us cannot begin to comprehend. Besides, I heard it's the name you were given in the Atlantian prophecies."

"I don't care. I'm Ivi or dragon-lady, to you, oh, leader of the realm."

"All right, all right, point taken. And I'll remain Flynn or... 'love of my life' to you."

Iviana snorted. "In your dreams."

When Flynn did not laugh quite as hardily as she had expected, she quickly changed the subject. "So, what else was decided in that meeting?"

"Oh, suggestions were made for new council members. What would you think of re-instating

Waymith? And Shynn seems quick. I already asked Jaela. She wasn't interested."

"No, I don't think Waymith will be interested for the same reason Jaela isn't. They want to focus on one another after having been apart so long. But I think Shynn would be wonderful... Aunt Shynn."

Flynn peered at her with a half-smile. "I'm having a hard time adjusting to it too, thinking of Necoli as your brother and all. I mean, what if you'd fallen—?"

"*Don't* even go there. Besides, the Great One would never have allowed it. It was His plan we met in the first place. Necoli needed us and now he's going to be reunited with his parents."

"Speaking of, have you heard from him and Nimua?"

"No!" Iviana cried, exasperated. "And are they in for a scolding, I'll tell you what. I sent that messenger the day before yesterday and after what they would have learned, I surely expected them to be back by now, at least to see Naii!"

"I'm sure they have a good reason," comforted Flynn.

Iviana made a face.

"Well, what do *you* think?" he asked.

"I think they've eloped!" she said with irritation.

"What's wrong with that?"

"Nimua is one of my best friends! I wanted to see her marry."

Flynn grew quiet at that and Iviana took comfort in knowing he understood.

"Well, you don't actually know if they have," he offered. "Perhaps they remained because they were needed for something. Your departure was unexpected and one of the villagers may have needed aid."

"I hadn't thought of that," she said, considering. "I wonder if I should have gone myself, instead of sending a messenger."

Flynn raised a brow. "You were a little busy. Besides, you're weak after the events of the glory-river. But listen, you haven't even given me a chance to ask my question yet."

Iviana hesitated. "And what is that?"

"Well... and I know what your reaction will be given your current plans, but give me a chance to finish."

"Oh, just spit it out, why don't you?"

"Fine. The council and I would dearly like to have you join us—on the council, that is."

Iviana opened her mouth, but he interrupted with, "I know, I know. You want to travel the globe. But all we ask is you attend whatever meetings you can and I absolutely promise things are going to be vastly different. Especially for you. I mean, I think if they thought you'd consent, they'd hoist me out and make *you* Realm Leader. Anyway, at least it would give you a chance to keep an eye on things. I might need you..."

"You don't need me, Flynn. All you need is the Great One."

"Well, in any case, we would all be honored if you would join us."

Iviana thought a while. This certainly hadn't been the question she'd expected, but she couldn't help feeling relieved. "I will think about it."

☙

It wasn't until the following day that the messenger Iviana had sent to Nimua and Necoli returned with news that made things abundantly clear: Necoli was severely ill and had been since the day Iviana and the others had left.

In Nimua's note, she mentioned how even the forest was ill and Iviana gathered the colder months had come upon Kierelia much sooner than they usually did. Likely, if Necoli had not anticipated this on their outing and the evening had grown cold, he had done what he could to keep Nimua warm and neglected himself.

A part of Iviana blamed herself for not waiting for them to return before she'd left, but from the sounds of it, they had gotten lost and had not returned until nightfall. Besides, so long as Iviana could get there, she knew she could more than handle things.

"We're coming with you," Darist said as he and Marquen entered her hut where she was throwing a few provisions together.

"Very well," she replied. "We will have to use the door to Jaela's Cavern, then. Her letter mentioned a dark dragon attack nearby, which means people will be on the lookout. I don't want to endanger ours."

"Will we just end up slowing you down?" Darist asked.

Iviana shook her head. "It will be fine. I'd like you with me."

So, the three swiftly made their way to the portal and sprinted through Jaela's Cavern. Upon exiting the tunnels, they were confronted by an older man waiting with three saddled horses, two brown and one a black stallion, all from Sir Retrom's estate.

Iviana was speechless. Not only was it unexpected, but it began to remind her of a dream she'd had some time ago, when she'd fallen asleep outside the Council Hall.

"Lady Laurel had a dream. Said you'd be needing these," explained the stable-hand. "I didn't expect you to actually be here."

Iviana thanked the man, but her mind raced as the three started toward FairGlenn. Not only did she suspect Flynn's sister was either a Seer or even a Dream-walker—which she would need to conceal more carefully living in Kierelia—but the dream she had recalled was coming back to her in full. At first, her stomach clenched so tightly, she thought she would burst with it, but the power that had produced the river was still inside of her, churning to life even now.

She had been correct in thinking the cold had come early, but she had not expected winter. As Nimua had never been in such a cold climate, Iviana hoped she had not grown ill as well, but she would not borrow trouble. Instead, she followed the leading of the power within.

And so it was, when the three drew into the village and were met by a young man who informed them her friends would not be at home, but were out in a nearby field, attending Necoli's funeral, she did not quake with the news.

"Iviana, I'm so sorry," Darist began with wide, teary eyes.

But Iviana silenced him with a movement of her hand. She would accept no pity. Instead, she turned her steed in the direction of the golden plain that sparkled with the early morning frost. At one point, she looked to Marquen and was met by a reassuring smile, as if he knew very well what she intended and had full confidence.

Before long, they caught sight of a group of mourners clothed in black. As the gathering noticed their approach, Nimua rushed to Iviana in tears. She was wailing something, but Iviana could not make out her words. Only the sound of her own heartbeat played in her ears as she recognized the urn in Nimua's arms.

Leaping from her horse, she embraced her friend. "Nimua... Nimua, hush," she soothed.

Nimua looked up into the face of her friend and took notice of what had caught Iviana's attention: the urn. "This is... *him*," she moaned pitifully. "He's gone..."

Iviana took hold of her shoulders and said with confidence, "No, he's not."

The tears in Nimua's eyes halted a moment as she studied Iviana. "You have changed," was all she could seem to say.

Iviana nodded. "Would you... would you mind pouring out the ashes for me?" she requested with compassion, knowing what it must seem she was asking.

At first, Nimua looked as if she would refuse, as if Iviana had asked something obscene. But then she peered into Iviana's eyes and studied them. Iviana watched as a number of thoughts played through her mind. Nimua had not been there to witness the glory-river; there was no reason for her to trust her, except that she *knew* her—knew her better than almost anyone. Therefore, she did as she was told, opening the urn and spilling the ashy remains of her love into the frigid air.

As the wind caught them in its clutches, tearing him far from them, Nimua's sobbing became guttural. But Iviana lay a hand upon her shoulder. Halting her wailing, Nimua listened as Iviana called them back in the name of the Anointed One and it was not long before the ashes returned in black swirling tendrils, gathering themselves into a blurred form.

"Iviana, wh-what is happening?" Nimua asked

breathlessly, the tears frozen on her face.

"Sorry, brother," spoke Iviana to the ashes. "We're not done with you just yet."

As the ashes completed Necoli's form, his color and solidity returned with a sudden inhalation of breath. Fervently, Nimua fell upon his feet, weeping loudly.

Iviana could hardly believe what she had done or, rather, what the Great One had done. She'd followed the leading of her dream from some time ago, as well as the urging in her heart, but she had moved as if possessed. Now it had actually been fulfilled, she wanted to fall upon his feet and weep as well.

Necoli appeared more than a little confused by the appearance of the would-be mourners, but it was obvious his most significant concern was reaching down to comfort the emotional woman at his feet. Iviana could only imagine he had some small inkling as to what had occurred, but doubted he truly understood.

She made ready to explain what the Great One had done for him, but at the sight of not only a dead man's ashes returning to life, but that very life actually *moving and breathing*, those who had attended the funeral swarmed Necoli, Nimua and

Iviana. Overcome with excitement, they pulled Iviana this way and that. It was only Darist's strength and Marquen's words that rescued her.

Once the people were settled, Iviana requested they keep the matter quiet, especially as she did not yet fully comprehend the situation herself. But by the rate at which they flew toward the village, she understood their intention. In truth, Iviana could not blame them. Though she had seen the marvelous power of the Great One in that glorious river, she had not yet anticipated it was capable of doing such a thing through her.

Once they were alone, Darist could only stare into her face with wide eyes, forcing Iviana to truly face what had transpired. She had taken the ashes of a dead man and spoken life back into them. It should not have happened and it would not have had it not been for that dream. Ultimately, it was altogether surreal.

"We have a lot of work to do, haven't we," said Marquen, both stunned and thrilled, "if we are to accomplish feats such as this."

Iviana nodded. The Great One was revealing Himself as not only powerful, but loving. For whatever reason, He was not finished with her brother and what a mercy it was. She could not have born losing him before revealing the truth about their connection. The Great One had already done so much for her in so many ways, but the result of her obedience had blessed her further. For, had she not returned for the prisoners, she would not have discovered Necoli's parents were alive and learned she had family. It was all a wonder to her, filling her heart with such love for the Ones who had made it all happen.

༄

By the following day, Iviana had returned to the Greater Archipelagos with her companions and reunited not only Nimua with her mother, but Necoli with the parents he had believed dead. That reunion had been more touching than even she had imagined, for not only had he thought them lost, but they had not parted on pleasant terms, each regretting their share. Since then, the Great One had worked in the three of them, creating room for a renewed bond.

As they heard the story of how Necoli had actually died and been cremated only the day before, they smothered him with renewed affection, as well as Iviana, who had been used to raise him. Of course, they had been there that day on the cannibal island, but they had not realized the extent of what Iviana yet held within her. Indeed, she was only beginning to understand herself.

Necoli and his parents continued to make their apologies and promises and filled one another in on their time apart, making plans for the future. All the while, Iviana sat back, waiting. She knew it was not her place to tell him the truth of their parentage, for he yet believed the parents before him his birth parents. It must be they who revealed their secret.

Even so, it overjoyed her to watch as he introduced Nimua to them and then revealed they were engaged. The room was full of warm embraces with this news and Shynn and Japha happily surrounded Nimua, asking her a variety of questions, attempting to learn all they could of the delightful young woman who had helped to heal their son's heavy, rebellious heart.

As the sun began to fade, plans were formed for the day of the wedding as well as the days that would follow. Though Iviana had hoped Necoli and Nimua would join her on the quest to travel the world and further disperse the Great One's glory-river, she soon learned she would be parted from them for a time. For Shynn and Japha meant to return to

Kierelia once again, to continue their mission, and Necoli and Nimua shared their desire to go along, their part sharing their knowledge of the Anointed One's sacrifice with the Kierelians.

Then, of course, Naii, Shynn and Japha relayed to the two all that had happened on the cannibal island, of the great river of glory and its affect, describing just how Iviana had appeared as she stood as a vessel for the great power that was affecting their planet.

Nimua and Necoli revealed they had already begun to feel a great presence filling them as they sat in that room with the four who had been there—how it seemed to be leaking from them, working its way into their spirits.

At last, the room grew quiet, and Iviana caught Shynn looking between hers and her brother before, "Necoli... your father and I have something we wish to speak to you about."

Quietly and rather more slowly than Iviana preferred, the two unfolded the tale they had told her and awaited his reaction. Amazingly, though it was a shock for him to learn they were not his birth parents, he revealed it had often felt as if it must be so. He could not say just why, that it was only a feeling. Finally, he asked who his birth parents had been.

Iviana caught her breath, nervous for the moment they would reveal all. Catching this, Necoli peered up at her questioningly, as if guessing the answer.

"Ivi, girl," he said. "Won't you tell me?"

Iviana felt she was ready to cry as she said, "They are my own, Redden and Tasia." Once finished, she held her breath, awaiting his response, but Nimua beat him to it.

"Iviana, you have a brother? How could you have let us sit here and talk all day without saying anything? No wonder you've been so quiet!" Silently, she took hold of Iviana's hand, as if sensing her nerves about Necoli's response.

As Necoli sat staring into Iviana's face, a few surprising tears fell from his eyes. "Well, that is rather wondrous. In the lowest moment of my life, the Great One led me not only to Nimua, the love of my life, but to my very own sister... and I have always wanted a sister."

"It's true!" Nimua shouted. "He told me he always dreamed of having a sibling to share good times with as a boy!"

Iviana finally allowed a small portion of her tears to fall as these two lost souls met truly for the first time.

"Won't you come back to Kierelia with us?" he asked, almost desperately, as if he, too, had only just found his family, though he had always had loving parents who were, after all, his own blood.

"I cannot," she admitted regretfully. "I have other plans—plans I had, in truth, hoped the two of you would help me with. However, I see clearly the Great One had plans of His own. He has called each of us to missions equally important, though, for now, in separate worlds."

ဆ21ဪ

ꟾVIANA

EARLY THE FOLLOWING morning, Iviana was busy packing for the journey ahead when Darist knocked on the wall from the back patio.

"Who is it?" she called.

"Your worst nightmare, I suspect," he replied easily.

Chuckling, Iviana invited him in and stopped her packing to sit on the swing that hung from her ceiling to offer her full attention.

"Have you come to say goodbye, then?" she asked, secretly hoping this was not so.

"You know, you have not even told me yourself what it is you plan to do," he said congenially, though she could tell he was hurt.

"I haven't? I had not realized. How stupid of me. The Great One has called me to travel the whole of the Greater Archipelagos and pour that river all over it."

"Well, that sounds spectacular," was his genuine reply.

Iviana nodded. "There's a fire started here, but there's a whole world that needs to be reached."

"And when you're finished here?"

"Kaern."

"And after that?"

Iviana grinned. "Who knows? I found out there was a world outside Kaern, in another dimension. Who knows how many more there are… waiting."

"So, you plan to go on until there's nothing left to reach?"

"Sure. Or until the Great One leads me into something else. Who knows?"

"I hear Marquen and Era are going with you."

"Yes, Era asked to come a few days ago and Marquen inquired the day before yesterday."

Darist smiled, then appeared on the verge of something before he finally blurted, "You, uh… you open to more company?"

"You mean you? Oh, no, thank you."

"Oh, that's all right, I just thought—"

Iviana could not resist laughing as she said, "I was only joking! Honestly, I was hoping you'd come."

"Honestly, I believe I'm supposed to. I think I was always supposed to; it's what I'm called to because... you know, *who knows?*" he said with eyes sparkling with mirth.

Iviana replied with a sparkle of her own and sent him off to pack.

☙

Iviana was late in appearing on the beach where she and the others were to depart. When she arrived, all her friends—those traveling with her and those there to bid them farewell—were already waiting. The sight of them nearly drew happy tears from her eyes, for she remembered her childhood days when she had known and loved but one person and now she had friends and even family who loved her and would be there for her through thick and thin, whatever was to come.

"Iviana!" called Nimua when she spotted her coming toward them.

At that moment, everyone turned to shower her with a variety of greetings, cheers and smiles, their warm welcome and affection giving her goosebumps. Oh, how sweet the Great One had been to her.

"Iviana, my dear girl," said Old Man Waymith, taking hold of her hands. "What can I possibly say to you, young woman?" He shook his head. His eyes, that had formerly been blind, were filled with emotion. "To think I had no idea who the little girl force feeding me would turn out to be."

Iviana laughed at this, recalling the sweet times they had shared before he'd been taken away from her. "Not only have you given me my own daughter back, but you've given me yet another, if you don't mind my saying so."

Iviana laughed and wiped the sudden tears from her eyes. "I don't mind one bit," she admitted and surrounded him with a warm embrace.

"Thank you, dear girl," he said, "for saving my life, for providing the river that gave me the use of my eyes and legs and for giving me a second chance worth living for."

Jaela nodded. "I thank you as well and so would all those who were imprisoned if they could be here. You have given us great hopes for the future. I think Jaela—*the* Jaela—would be pleased by what you have done for the world that had been a precious gift to her."

This was growing to be almost too much for

Iviana, so she pleaded, "Oh, please, no more of these wonderful words, you two. I really cannot bear it and there are too many people here to see me cry."

She warmly embraced each of them before turning to where Nimua stood with Naii, Necoli, Shynn and Japha. By these, she was drenched in kisses, hugs and tender words. Her aunt and uncle, it seemed, having missing out on adopting her along with Necoli, meant to do so now as much as they could and treated her as if she was their own.

And, of course, Naii had long been a mother-figure, offering unwavering support. Doing no different now, she pulled Iviana aside and offered her words of encouragement, making Iviana promise to return to the Isle of Dragons as often as she could so she could catch glimpses of her courageous girl. The mention of that nickname reminded Iviana of what Naii's own mother used to call her. Telling Naii so, the woman broke down in tears, making room for Necoli and Nimua to step in while she gathered herself.

"You'll remember our deal then, won't you?" Nimua said to her.

"Deal?" Iviana asked quizzically.

Nimua pulled her close. "You're supposed to come around so often my husband will tire of you.

Of course, now he's your brother, I don't suppose he'll mind quite so much."

Iviana turned to Necoli with a smirk. "He'd better not. We're parting so soon, we'll have plenty of catching up to do."

"Like building tree-houses and playing knights and rogues, not to mention stealing chickens and raiding storehouses."

Iviana raised a brow at him. "We obviously had very different childhoods, pirate."

"Oh, yes, there's that. We've got to run away and join a crew of pirates. Though, since I already did, I suppose it's your turn."

Iviana shook her head, but replied, "Sounds like an adventure."

"Oh, Ivi," Nimua said as she took hold of her hands. "I cannot believe I'm going to be in your world while you're staying here in mine. It is terribly unfair. Even so, I'm eager for what's in store for you. Darist had better take good care of you," she added when he drew up to the group.

"Oh, that's why I'm going. Someone's got to keep this girl in line," he said, lightly tugging on Iviana's hair.

True to form, Nimua punched Darist in the arm, saying, "More like you'll be so troublesome she'll have to send you back to us before she's half through."

The three friends laughed together, sharing memories, when Chamaeleo suddenly appeared in their midst.

"Pardon the intrusion, but I would rather like to steal our Chosen One away for a moment."

"Oh, no, you don't, gran," said Necoli. "She's *my* sister, after all."

Chamaeleo proceeded to pinch his cheek, saying, "Well, if I'm your grandmother, that makes her my grandchild too. So, I've just as much right as you have, laddie." With that, she led Iviana away

"Where did you come from?" Iviana asked. "I haven't seen you since that day in Kierelia and here it sounds as if you knew about me and Necoli all along. Aren't you happy to find Shynn and Japha alive?"

"Of course, but I've already seen them. I'm sorry I didn't have time to search you out as well, but you've been an awfully busy girl what with raising people from the dead and all. As far as my knowledge of your relationship to Necoli, I really had no idea who your parents were until I met with your aunt and uncle, so no accusing me of keeping any more secrets than I already have.

"Now, speaking of secrets, I wanted to thank

you… for being all I dreamed you'd be when I was young and, oh, so lost."

Iviana was taken aback by these words. "What do you mean?"

"When I was that young girl who'd just lost her parents, alone in a world I knew very little about, you were the one the Great One used to give me hope. He told me you'd one day make it possible for me to return home and be accepted and safe among my own people."

"But, you don't even need their acceptance anymore, do you?" asked Iviana.

"I don't… but I would still like to have it. It is a luxury to be able to live *safely* among the people of my childhood home. Of course, I'm not certain how often I'll be here, but I will see you around as often as I am able.

"In any case, my point in speaking with you is this: when I was at my lowest point, you were the hope I clung to, the one I ventured to be like even as I have grown into a daft old woman who wears the face of a young one. And that has not changed. You have returned that little girl's beautiful home to her, and for that I thank you."

Iviana was overcome by these words. Chamaeleo was one of the most impressive women she knew. To hear that visions of herself were what had inspired Chamaeleo to be all that she was, was incredible.

Chamaeleo's attention was suddenly caught by something and Iviana strained to discover what it was, but then Chamaeleo took firm hold of her arm and pointed to where Era stood surrounded by her parents and friends.

"Keep an eye on that one," she said.

Iviana was stunned by her earnestness. "Why do you say that?"

"Because, well, I promised I would not say and so I cannot. I suppose this is why my mother told me never to give my word. It is *ever* so inconvenient."

"Chamaeleo, you're doing it again—telling me something, but not telling. I'd really hoped we were beyond that by now."

Chamaeleo looked deep into her face, as if fighting herself. At last, she blurted out, "Just... keep an eye on her... but not too close or else, well, the Great One only knows."

With that, she disappeared, probably taking the form of one of the sandy granules at her feet. Iviana shrugged off her irritation and gazed at Era where she was bidding her parents a tearful farewell... and wondered.

"So, you are really and truly leaving us," Flynn said from behind her.

Iviana turned to face him. "I was afraid you weren't coming. Thought I would have to drop in with Tragor and let him have his way with you once and for all."

"*That* is something I truly fear," he said with a glimmer of humor, though it was apparent he recalled how little Tragor cared for him.

"But listen," Iviana said more seriously. "I am not leaving. I'll be *here*, in the Greater Archipelagos. Besides, you know I must do this. How long it will take, I do not know, but I'll be back now and then. Naii made me promise."

Flynn studied her as he said, "Yes, I know your plans. They are beautiful. I only wish I could come with you."

This pained Iviana, for she had been wishing the same. "I know, but I'll be back soon to tell you of all my adventures."

"Fine. Then I will keep as busy as possible until then."

Iviana grinned. "You darling boy, I will miss you. And I'll send letters as often as I am able."

It was then Darist and Marquen called to her, informing the dragons had arrived.

Flynn released a slow, sad but proud smile. It was obvious there was a great deal of thinking done behind it, but he said simply, "Fly back to me soon, dragon-savior."

As the gathering on the beach helped them pack their belongings onto the dragons, the final farewells were made until at last the four were seated on the creatures who were to carry them through their journey, Tragor taking his proud stance at the head of them. Though he was old, he was more than ready for the adventures in store, Iviana knew. He had played the hermit after Latos' death long enough. It was time for him to truly live again.

Peering down at the sea of waving hands, Iviana batted the tears from her eyes and looked toward the blazing sun that was calling her and the others forward, urging them to fulfill the destiny the Great One had planned before their very existence.

An Afterword from Era

I HAVE SEEN the future. Admittedly, it was the reason I desired to travel with the woman who is one day to be my mother. I have traveled and witnessed how heartbroken she will be on the day that we are parted and I think, when I tell her all, it would hurt her if I chose to miss these next years with her before I am born. I hope we may be able to make up the time that will be lost... or for me the time that has already been lost. I think it is what the Great One intended, that in losing me, she would yet find me. In losing me, she will not have truly lost me at all. For from now on, I will always be with her.

It took me some time to understand why the Great One chose to send me into the past that I would be there when she would have to make that great decision—the decision that would affect the world. The answer is this: without me and my knowledge of the future, she would not have returned. Why else should *I*, of all people, have seen the future? And why was I, Iviana's daughter, chosen for the task? It is because we have a connection she could not ignore, though it is a connection she does not yet understand.

But, you see, there was so much more entailed in my decision than simply gaining lost years, for I have heard of the wonders that will be seen wherever the Glory-bringer goes and it will be more breathtaking than what we have already seen. In truth, I have seen even beyond her years—the years birthed of what she produced in the name of the Great One—and it will be *spectacular.* When I found myself with the opportunity to be a part of planting those seeds, laying the ground work and seeing wonders, what else could I do?

Of course, I cannot tell all, but this I will say: The cannibal island will one day be called "The City of His Glory." Iviana will be forever honored as the Glory-bringer and a statue of her likeness will be placed beside the one of our grandfather, Latos. I was surprised to learn that I am also to be remembered for something that I have yet to do and do not yet understand, but that is as it should be. I am not one for spoiled secrets.

Furthermore, the wounded, sick and dying who enter the river at the center of that island will continue to receive healing and it is said that at certain hours, when all is quiet and the wind blows just right, one can hear music playing from its depths, sounding as if from another world—even, perhaps, that of the Great One's Paradise. And should one gaze into the river in that moment, they may even glimpse unusual creatures dancing to its tune.

I would also like to note that Aedis and Merrick still marry in this time-line. It seems they are truly destined for one another, despite my utter confusion on the matter. However, their futures are so much more brilliant and glamorous than they might have been had Iviana not fulfilled her destiny. In fact, had she not, they might never have unlocked the secret of the portals and they would never have helped us discover so many other worlds. But that is a tale for another time.

A NOTE FROM THE AUTHOR

As humans formed by the hands of a creative, imaginative God, we crave the supernatural. Believe it or not, we yearn for the very power we are actually *destined* for. It is why media concerning magic, witchcraft and sorcery is so prevalent today, because we were born for greater planes than most of us have currently seen.

Amazingly, we are actually created to work in the same supernatural powers displayed in the bible and we are feeling the lack of it as our culture turns to crafty, counterfeit imitations. Though there are a few who perform miraculous acts around the world, the rest of us are left leading considerably mundane lives in a compromised condition, as if in half-form.

Nevertheless, we *are* sons and daughters made in

the image of an all-powerful God Who longs to see us live as supernatural kingdom-beings who have claimed their birthright and are moving in signs and wonders to lead a generation to Him. Assuredly, it is possible to manifest God's glory through His great power in order to heal the wounded, sick and dying and bring hope and life to people who are dry and desolate.

One day, it may even be possible to breathe underwater without scuba gear or fly without aviation. As for seeking, that is a gift accessible to anyone. Seek God, soak up His presence and you will find all that you long for, completing the destiny He planned for you before you were formed in your mother's womb.

My question is this: Do you long to move in the supernatural? If yes, the answer is simple. Seek. Seek Him. *He is waiting.*

Furthermore...

I know there are many books out there to choose from, so I would like to thank you for following Iviana's journey in the Seeker's Trilogy. If you enjoyed this book, please consider leaving a review to let like-minded readers know they might enjoy it too. To connect with me, you can visit any of the following sites. I would love to hear from you!

CassandraBoyson.com

Facebook.com/CassandraBoyson

Twitter.com/CassandraBoyson

Or find me on Goodreads.com

Made in the USA
Middletown, DE
18 December 2016